THE NAKED TROCAR

with

THE BEST REVENGE

THE NAKED TROCAR

A Not-So-True Crime Novel

with

THE BEST REVENGE

A Sort-Of Western

by

Fender Tucker

RAMBLE HOUSE

To Bill, Marcia, Dick, Pat and Ed

And especially, Naomi

ISBN 13: 978-1-60543-16-4

ISBN 10: 1-60543-016-1

CONTENTS

THE NAKED TROCAR

A NOT-SO-TRUE CRIME NOVEL

PROLOGUE: The Murder

The Jaynes Mortuary stood at the end of a dead end road in Shiprock New Mexico. It was in a residential area and the words "Jaynes Mortuary" in red neon script was the only light on the short street. It was an adobe building, one story with a basement, and if it weren't for the neon, no one would ever have any reason for going to the end of the road—except for a death in the family.

One night in late 1983, if you had been standing in the street outside the mortuary, you would have seen the door open, yellow light spilling out over the cactus and sand that made up the yard of the building. You would have seen a young man, perhaps a Navajo boy, run out of the door with the shadow of a larger person looming in the doorway. You may have even heard a sobbing shout from either the boy or the shadow before seeing what looked like a gun in the hand of the man in the doorway.

You would have then heard the sound of a gunshot and seen the young boy sprawl to the ground, obviously shot in the back. The man, who remained only a shadow, would then move to the boy, and either put into or take something from the pocket of the boy's shirt, before going back into the building.

And the sobbing would have continued until the door closed and the neon light was all you could see.

But you weren't there back in 1983. Someone else was, but be thankful it wasn't you.

CHAPTER ONE: A Vacation in Farmington

As you approach Farmington New Mexico from the east on Highway 64 there's a time of day when you are for all intents and purposes clinically blind. The setting sun sits right on the highway ahead of you and as you pass by the turnoff that used to go to the Mesa Drive-In, about five miles east of the Animas River bridge, you have to slow down to ten miles an hour and hope no one stops in front of you—or doesn't stop in back of you. They're as blind as you are.

There's a clue to who and what I am in that description above. I grew up in Farmington in the 50s and even though there are, in 1989, numerous roads that split off of Highway 64 to the right and left, in my mind there's only the one turnoff—to the long-gone Mesa Drive-In. All of my memories of the town are from 1950 to 1967 when I used to own the place, or at least thought I did.

Farmington was an oil-field burg of maybe 5000 people back in the early 50s, growing to 15,000 by the time I got out of high school and left in 1965 to go to college in Las Cruces, downstate, then the army in the late 60s. I've lived in Cruces ever since, playing guitar in bar bands for a living and generally living the easy life. I could have stayed in Farmington and played but Las Cruces, as a university town, was better for surviving in the sleazy bar bidness.

Now, in 1989, Farmington is a sprawling hotbed of traffic, covering three times the area that it did in the 50s, and full of people I don't know. Needless to say, I liked it better back when I lived there.

We all go back to our home towns sooner or later and I was on a vacation, which meant that a week-long gig we had slated at a nifty bar in Ruidoso up in the mountains had been cancelled at the last minute. So the other members of The Mighty Calhoon Brothers and I had all decided to take advantage of the lack of work—and pay—and go on separate vacations. I, Knees, went to Farmington; Balls (who claims to have taken his nickname as a tribute to Honoré de Balzac) went home to Clovis; and Thyroid (who wasn't too thrilled about adopting a body-part nickname and was having medical trouble with his thyroid gland at the time) visited his folks in Belen.

That's me, Knees Calhoon, guitar picker and slugabed, and the one who's going to tell you all about my fateful vacation in Farmington this fall of 1989.

It was a Monday evening when I drove into town, blinded by the sun and tired from the seven-hour drive from Las Cruces. I had no plans for how long I would stay, or where. I didn't know very many people who were still in Farmington and none of them were anyone I could call and stay with. So I decided to stay at one of the old motels on Main Street, ones that were there in 1950 when my family, my mother, father and little brother Billy, moved to town in 1950. It made me feel good that there were a few places from the old days still around, maybe because none of my family was. My father had died in the late 50s, my mother in the 70s and Billy had been killed in '83.

The sun finally went down and traffic picked up a bit as I crossed the Animas River and drove along Broadway before turning north to Main Street at Wall Street. The Arrowhead Motel loomed on the south side of Main just as it had back in 1950 when it was at the very end of town. It looked a little bigger than I remembered and had a huge neon sign with a marquee that blared that it was "100% American owned". That's a clue to something, too, but I don't know what.

I pulled in and paid $80 for a room for four nights. It was a typical motel room, TV with bad cable, a reasonable king-size bed and a working air conditioner. I took off my shoes and pants and leaned back on the bed and flipped on the TV. I had rolled a dozen joints for the trip, hoping that would last me, and smoked one while watching the news. It was the same old Reagan bullshit and I was glad that I had a compartmentalized life back in Las Cruces where I could ignore the beginning of the end of American civilization at the hands of a clueless ham actor.

I was used to going out every night to work so around nine o'clock I took a shower, got dressed and went to the El Charro Restaurant on west Main, a Mexican place I used to like in the old days. It was still there and the hot sauce was as sweat-producing as ever. Great enchiladas, too. Right next to it was the El Vasito Lounge, where I had learned the ropes of the sleazy bar scene back in 1966. It was disappointing to see that it had been renamed The Maverick Club but it was still a pretty good C&W bar and I watched a band from Texas play a decent set before heading back to the motel.

I had no idea of what I was going to do in my old home town. I felt about as lost as I had ever felt in my life.

CHAPTER TWO: Reminiscence

I can't—and don't—complain about my childhood. Farmington was a perfect place to grow up back in the 50s when Eisenhower was our national grandfather and the oil fields were booming. I had my bicycle and could go anywhere in town, or even out of town. Once you reached the edge of town in any direction, you ran into incredible desert scenes with cacti, sand and magnificent sandstone formations. You didn't have to get in a car and drive for hours to be in the middle of the stinkin' desert; you could walk or bike there. And Billy and I did.

My family had friends who lived out by the new country club on Highway 550 halfway to Aztec and that's where we did most of our desert exploring. We'd take canteens full of water and sandwiches and spend the whole day exploring and hiking out there, watching out for rattlesnakes and scorpions, running up and down the sandstone with total abandon. On days we went west instead of east, there was the La Plata highway that led north to Colorado and Mancos. There was a side road that paralleled the La Plata highway that led to a girl scout's campground and it was one of our favorite hiking areas. It was full of canyons and miniature cliffs like the Anasazi cliffs of Mesa Verde or Canyon de Chelly—but without the dwellings—and we knew them as well as we knew the streets of Farmington.

Chokecherry Canyon was about two miles up the side road. It was where the high school students had their beer bashes on weekend nights. The canyon was small, just a cul-de-sac off the left side of the road, but it was hidden from the road and perfect for the bonfires that the high school parties were centered around. Just behind the campfire area was a 20-foot cliff up to a mesa, and in this cliff was the notorious Fat Man's Misery, a tunnel in the base of the cliff that led up to the top—*if* you were man enough to climb it. Billy and I had been up Fat Man's Misery many times. We even climbed it in the dark. It opened on top of the mesa where you could get back down to road level by walking around the edge of the cliffs—about a half mile walk. It was practically impossible to climb down Fat Man's Misery. We tried it and just about killed ourselves.

To the south of town were the Bluffs, tall rugged cliffs that overlooked the San Juan River that skirted Farmington on the south. We even climbed the Bluffs one day when we were feeling specially energetic.

It was a great time to be alive and in Farmington and we made the most of it. It was because of these experiences in the desert that I decided to visit Farmington in 1989 on a whim.

Billy was one year younger than I was and we were inseparable in our younger days. Our father died when we were in our early teens and we found the freedom invigorating. As the oldest boy I was given the reins of the family by my mother and we all worked hard to get by, but the combination of freedom and responsibility, especially after I learned the guitar and started making a living in a band, made us grow up fast and happy.

Then, in 1967 I was drafted into the army and Billy joined the navy. Afterwards, I ended up in Las Cruces going to college on the GI Bill and Billy went back to Farmington where he lived with some friends from high school. We kept in touch with occasional letters and phone calls and I came back to town for the funeral in 1975 when our mother died.

Billy worked at a few places in Farmington and Shiprock, a small Navajo town thirty miles to the west, and then in 1983 his body was found just south of the

Bluffs in the oilfield area known as the Bisti. He had been shot in the back and his body hidden in the desert. It was only a fluke that a couple of Navajo boys had found him and the investigation had gone nowhere. I had driven up at the time but there was nothing I could do. I talked to several people who knew him well but they were all puzzled by the killing. He wasn't into heavy drugs or crime, that they knew of, and had no enemies.

Maybe Billy was the reason why I hadn't visited Farmington in more than six years.

I woke up late the next morning at the Arrowhead and wondered what I was going to do. I got dressed, smoked a half a joint and decided to go hunt down some breakfast.

I wanted to eat at some place that I remembered from back in the 50s.

CHAPTER THREE: Breakfast at the Avery

I drove west on Main looking at all the buildings. The traffic was not too heavy downtown and I was able to gawk at the old familiar places: Farmington Lumber Company, Harmony House, Li'l Diner, Snooker 8 Pool Hall—which will probably outlive its cockroaches—Noel Hardware, Harry's Bar, Allen Theater, Totah Theater, and finally, on the northwest corner of Main and Behrend, the Avery Hotel.

On the ground floor in the back was a great greasy spoon restaurant which had been there as long as I could remember. I saw a parking spot on Behrend right next to the side entrance to the restaurant and turned north onto Behrend then made a quick U-turn just past the empty space and pulled in directly behind a huge automobile with double tires on the back. As I got out of my 1969 Volkswagon Squareback, gray with carburetors instead of fuel injection, I noticed that the big vehicle was actually a hearse. On the side of it was printed in a flowery script "Jayne's Mortuary" and in smaller letters, "The Mortuary at the End of the Dead End Road".

What kind of an advertising mind thought of that one, I wondered as I put some coins in the parking meter and went inside the Avery Hotel.

It was brightly lit and looked about the same as I remembered it. I hoped the food was the same. I sat down at a booth facing the back of the restaurant and checked out the menu. Looked familiar.

As I was waiting for the waitress to take my order—huevos rancheros with fry bread and iced tea—I noticed a guy who was standing in an enclosed phone booth at the back of the restaurant. He looked vaguely familiar and as I looked more closely it hit me. Marty Jaynes. That's right, he owned the mortuary in Shiprock. That must be his hearse outside.

Marty and I went to school together. At least we started out together. We were the same age but he flunked one year around the fifth grade and was always a year behind me after that. He was more friends with Billy than with me. I didn't really know him that well back in school and had only run into him occasionally since then. There was some trouble Marty had with the law a few years back but I couldn't quite remember what it was.

I saw him take out a pen and write something on the wall of the booth just as the waitress took my order. I was wondering if I was going to say hi to Jaynes or not as she scooted off and he hung up the phone. He opened the door of the booth and looked straight at me as he exited. A look of recognition came over his face and he smiled and walked over to my booth.

"Hey, it's Tommy Calhoon," he said and put out his hand for me to shake. "What are you doin' in town?"

His hand was clammy and wrinkled and I didn't want to think why. He was about six feet tall and was probably a few pounds more than my 180. He had ridiculous curly hair, cut long in front even though it was thinning elsewhere. He sat down across the table from me.

"Marty Jaynes. It's good to see you. I'm going by Knees these days. Fact, I've been Knees ever since junior high."

"I know that. I was just goin' way back to when we were getting' slapped around by the nuns. God, those were the days. I'm surprised we survived."

I guess he saw something in my eyes that made him say quickly, "A'course not everybody survived, huh?" He looked a little embarrassed and continued, "So what're you doin' these days? Still pickin' the guitar?"

"Yeah, down in Las Cruces still. I hardly ever make it back to Farmington any more. I barely reco'nize the place now that's it's all overgrown and—"

"You said it! Downtown it's not so bad because most of the bidness's moved out on the highway to Aztec or the highway to Shiprock. That's where I spend most of my time, at the mortuary in Shiprock. The undertaking bidness never seems to die out."

I wasn't sure I wanted to talk about the "undertaking bidness" so I didn't acknowledge his strained joke and said, "Yeah, I saw your hearse outside. Uh, you eatin'?" Pointing at the menu.

He shook his head and said, "No, thanks, not now. So what brings you to Farmington?"

The waitress brought my food and we talked for about ten minutes, about the music business in Cruces, the state of the world, and a bit about the mortuary trade that wasn't too graphic for the huevos. It was when he mentioned that he had been away from the business for a few years that I remembered more about his legal troubles. He had gone to prison for manslaughter, or murder, or something.

I was curious and interrupted his discourse on the tools of the embalming arts and asked, "By the way, Marty, don't let me tread on any corns, but didn't you have a bit of trouble with the law in recent years?"

"Oh yeah. Fact, I went to prison for five goddam years. It was back in 1983 and it was for manslaughter, technically. I shot a guy who was stealing from me."

I don't know why I probed but it seemed like something I should know. And if I could get it from the horse's mouth. . .? "Stealing, huh?" I prompted.

"Well, there was this young Navajo kid named Sammy Arthur who worked for me at the mortuary. I had just opened up the Shiprock place and he ran errands, helped out with the embalmings, nothing too technical. I noticed that things were missing about two months before the incident but they were small stuff and I overlooked it. But then he started taking things that were, well, expensive and in a few cases, embarrassing—"

"Embarrassing? What do you mean?"

"Well, you know, like things that people put on the corpses. The Navajos are very superstitious about death and the disposition of the body. They have all sorts of taboos that I have to worry about and frankly, most of them don't make a lick a' sense."

"Wow. I can imagine. So what happened with the young boy, Sammy—"

"Arthur. Well, one night I confronted him about it and he got all freaked out and said he was going to go to the cops and tell them I was doin' all sorts of illegal things out there. I tried to keep him from leaving but he got out the front door and I had a gun and, well, there was a witness and she said that I shot him from the doorway as he was runnin' away."

"A witness?"

"It was a lady that lived in the house closest to the mortuary. It's set way back from the road so you hardly notice it but she apparently had a good view of the front of the mortuary and she said that I pointed the gun at him and shot him as he ran away. The jury believed her and I was given ten years for manslaughter. I got out in five for good behavior."

"How did you manage manslaughter? That sounds like maybe murder two." I was thinking I was going too far with this, but for some reason didn't care.

Jaynes said, "They found a medallion in his pocket which was supposed to have been buried with a body the week before. I also told them that he had threatened me with a trocar right before I shot him and that I was fearful for my life."

"Trocar? What's that?"

"It's a tool we use for embalming. Come on out to the plant—I call it 'the plant' 'cause that's what we do with the bodies—and I'll show you one."

"Hmmmm. Lemme take a rain check on that. But the shot in the back. How could they get around that?"

"Well, I *did* get ten years. Ol' Judge Slinger made sure I did time."

"Judge Slinger. Lawrence Slinger. I remember that name. God, he's been around for a long time, hasn't he? Hangin' judge, right?"

"It depends. I'm out now. On parole, keepin' my nose clean, workin' at the old job and sendin' a lot of Navajos off to the happy hunting grounds in the style they want. It's a living."

"I understand completely. We all gotta pay our dues."

I don't exactly know what made me uneasy about the conversation with Jaynes. It was nothing explicit in his words, but I felt that he was feeling me out as much as I was pumping him. I was curious about his homicidal experience and he wanted to know what I was doing in Farmington. He seemed almost suspicious about why I was in town, but why should he care?

We talked a bit more then Jaynes got up and said, " 'Scuse me a second. I gotta make a phone call." He walked to the booth and closing the door made a call. It was short and he came back to the table a couple of minutes later. We talked for another five minutes or so and I finished my meal and got up and shook hands with him as we said parting phrases. He handed me a card and said, "Here's my number. Hold it, that's an old number. Here's the new one." He took out a pen and wrote his phone number, in bright blue ink, on the card, crossing out the old one.

I walked to the cash register and paid the bill and Marty saluted me as he walked out the door onto Behrend.

I followed soon after—to find that I was being given a parking ticket.

I quickly glanced at the meter and saw that there were still fifteen minutes left. There were two cops, a man and a woman; the woman bedecked in full police regalia, hat, badge, crisp black uniform with all of the accessories, the man in civilian clothes but with a badge on his belt, highly visible. The woman had a nametag: Molly Miller.

Marty had moved on up to the hearse, which was directly in front of my Squareback, and was watching us.

"What seems to be the problem, officer?" I said to the woman officer and she looked up from her pad to ask me, "Is this your vehicle, sir?"

"Yes, it is."

"Well, it's illegally parked and I'm writing you up a citation. You can mail in the payment or, if you dispute this ticket, appear in court at the Municipal Courthouse, on, uh," she looked on another sheet of paper on her clipboard and continued, "Wednesday, that's tomorrow, at one p.m."

"What exactly is my crime here, officer?"

"You're parked too far away from the curb. The city ordinance states that the tires should be no more than 18 inches away from the curb. Yours are 20.5 inches. I'm afraid you are in violation of the ordinance."

I looked at my VW, which is a relatively narrow car. There were white lines painted on the asphalt, showing the boundaries of the parking spot for each meter. My car's outer tires were about two inches *inside* the white lines.

The two policemen looked at what I was looking at. Then I walked behind my car and stared at it, noticing that my car did not extend out into the street any further than the hearse in front of it did. In fact, the outer wheels of the hearse were on top of the white line showing the outer perimeter of the parking space. The two policemen saw what I was looking at.

I started to say something but there was a smirk on the detective's face that stopped me. This was not the time to argue. They wanted to give me a ticket. I kept my mouth shut and took the ticket and signed it when the woman handed it to me. The detective was walking around my car peering into the windows, not even trying to be coy about it. Jaynes sat behind the wheel of the hearse but hadn't started it yet.

The two cops, who were parked on the opposite side of the street in a No Parking zone got in their car and started it, talking on their car phone. On the side of the police car it read, "To Serve and Protect".

I was pissed off and frustrated and not sure if I was being railroaded or not—and for reasons I knew not enough about. Something was off-balance here. So instead of driving off in a huff, I walked back into the restaurant, leaving my car parked illegally. To hell with 'em. I looked around the restaurant and then decided what to do. I walked to the left out of the restaurant's inner doors to the lobby of the hotel and exited the front of the Avery Hotel and walked to the corner of the building on Behrend street. I peeked around the corner and saw that the hearse was still in front of my car and that the cop car had pulled out and was parked next to the hearse—blocking traffic going south on Behrend if there had been any—and the detective was talking animatedly with Jaynes, who was still behind the wheel of the hearse. They were almost yelling at each other and I heard the dick say something like, "Don't take any chances. Take him out of you need to."

And Jaynes answered, "Okay, okay. Easy for you to say."

Then they mumbled for a while longer and I thought I heard a word that ended in "—inger". Finger? Ringer? Slinger? Judge Slinger?

The cop car pulled away and I quickly turned around and scooted back inside the front doors of the Avery Hotel. I walked back to the restaurant and went to the side door and looked out to see that the hearse had gone too.

I was perplexed and didn't know what to think. How much would the ticket be for? Probably just a few bucks. It was a non-moving parking violation. But there seemed to be a conspiracy of some sort between the cops and Jaynes. I wanted to know more. And even though there was nothing that directly connected what was going on in Farmington here in 1989 with what happened in 1983, I had a nagging hunch deep down that kept poking at my mind.

I had an idea. I went to the phone booth at the back and entered it and closed the door. Good. There was a phone book. I looked up "Lawyers" in the yellow pages and then moved to "Attorneys" as instructed. Maybe Barney is still in town, I thought. I thumbed through the five pages of lawyers and spotted what I was looking for: "Eastwick, Barney, criminal law."

I called the number and got a secretary, who took my name and put me on hold. A few seconds later a big voice boomed through the phone, "Knees Calhoon! You old git-picker. What're you doing in Sin City?" It was unmistakably Barney Eastwick, a flamboyant lawyer I knew from college in Las Cruces. He'd gone on to law school and ended up practicing in Farmington. I'd last seen him a decade before when he helped me get my divorce.

"I'm just in town for a vacation. No reason whatsoever. Thought I'd see how the place had changed without my presence. I trust you're doing okay?"

"Oh I'm just havin' fun with the law. In this town it's a racket and I'm swingin' it for all I'm worth. Don't tell me you need a lawyer!"

"Well, actually, Barney, I do. It's not a big deal, just a parking ticket but I think there are, uh, facets to it that might make it worth your interest. It involves an ordinance that makes no sense and a couple of cops who are itching to follow that ordinance to the letter. I think we can beat the rap and maybe even humiliate a couple of asshole cops at the same time."

"That sounds pretty good. I always enjoy stickin' it to Farmington's finest when they get too pompous. When's your court date?"

"It's tomorrow at one p.m. Can you swing that? I wouldn't think it would take much time to plead the case."

"There's nothing like goin' into court without knowin' what the case is about. It's the ultimate high wire act for us legal folks."

"Well, hell, I can tell you what it's all about before the case. No need to walk the wire without a net. How about if I come to your office tomorrow at noon and we go over it and then drive over to the Municipal Court and confront the formidable Molly Miller and her mufti-clad consort?"

"Huh? Mufti-clad? You must mean Detective Smuff. Wally Smuff. He and Miller are well-known partners in crime here in town. Molly 'n' Wally. They always ride together. I would *love* to chop off a few inches a' those two. One tomorrow afternoon, eh? That's sounds good. You don't wanna tell me a bit more about what I'll be arguin'?"

"I have complete confidence you'll snap to the best defense right away. We can discuss it tomorrow. I'll see you at noon?"

"Okay. See you then, Knees."

As I hung up the phone I happened to glance up on the wall of the booth and saw, in bright blue ink, "Thur. 10:30, mort." That wasn't too hard to figure out, even whether it was a.m. or p.m. I had a feeling that whatever Jaynes was up to, it was not happening at 10:30 in the morning. Tomorrow night at 10:30 at the mortuary.

I left the restaurant, got in my illegally parked Squareback—whose meter read 'VIOLATION' in big red letters by now—and drove back to the Arrowhead Motel. I needed to smoke a joint and think things over. I could only take so much service and protection.

After watching a damn good Robert Mitchum western in the motel room I took a nap and later had dinner at Chef Bernie's Restaurant out on the west side of town. I did a little more sightseeing then I checked out the Office Bar on East Main. The band was decent but I couldn't get the wrongness of the ticket and Jaynes and the cops out of my head. Maybe I was anticipating having my day in court with a mouthpiece like Barney Eastwick.

I made it back to the Arrowhead by eleven, smoked a joint and watched a horror flick about a giant mollusk that was eating nubile swimmers. Pretty good, actually. Then I started reading a David Dodge paperback I'd brought along and crapped out after a couple of chapters.

So ended my first full day back in my home town.

CHAPTER FOUR: The Trial

Barney Eastwick's office was a half block north of Main on Orchard in a refurbished old two-story brick house, and I got there a little after high noon. We had to get up to the court on Municipal Drive, by the airport, so I knew we only had a half-hour or so for me to fill him in on the case. It should be easy.

I had started the day with a terrific lunch/breakfast at the Li'l Diner just a few blocks down Main Street, then walked up and down the length of the downtown area seeing what kind of books I could find. That's what I did when in a strange town, and even though I still knew the geography, I was finding Farmington strange. Don's News Stand, the combo newsstand/ book store/pinball alley of my youth was now a Navajo Trinket store. No 25 cent Gold Medal books to be found in 1989. But there was a damn good paperback store next to the Allen Theater, which had once been a second pool hall on Main Street back in the 60s. How many towns of less than 15,000 people could brag of having *two* pool halls on Main Street? And the weird thing is that for about a year back in 1965 there was a third pool hall, Singleton's, right off Main on Commercial Street.

After I made it back to the Arrowhead and had a quick smoke, I was ready to consult my lawyer.

I parked behind the Snooker 8 Pool Hall and found my way up to his office on the second floor. It was a spacious room, with books lining the walls and a huge polished wood desk in the center. Barney, a big guy who was a little balder than I'd remembered him, shook hands with me and pointed me to a comfortable chair.

"So, Knees Calhoon, you slink back into town and immediately antagonize the men in blue. That sounds about right."

"I didn't actually slink, but you can bet next time I will. Barney, you're looking good. I guess the legal life agrees with you. Are you up for a Supreme Court-worthy case, full of sound and fury?"

"I thought you said it was a parking violation?"

"Bad parkers are people, too. But here's the case in a nutshell. I got a ticket for parking 20.5 inches away from the curb in my VW Squareback, even though my car was *completely* within the white lines that described the perimeter of the parking spot. The ordinance states that the near tires must be within 18 inches."

"Hmmm. Sounds like a typical stupidly thought out law. You propose that I argue that the purpose of the law is to keep people from sticking out in traffic too far, and that a better measurement would be from the *far* wheels to the curb?"

"Damn, Barney! You sure picked the right career. That's *exactly* what I think the argument should be. But I even have some more corroborating evidence of the argument, if the cops and Marty Jaynes don't outright lie—"

"Marty Jaynes? What the hell does he have to do with this?"

"Nothing, really. He was just parked in his hearse right in front of me and even though he was sticking out into traffic about 6 inches more than I was, because he was parked closer to the curb, he didn't get a ticket."

Barney Eastwick paused a moment, rubbed his hands together and said, "So let me get this straight. Molly Miller and Wally Smuff are giving you a ticket and Marty Jaynes is there in his hearse. Did he say anything?"

"Well, not really. I had talked a bit with Jaynes in the Avery Hotel restaurant before the ticket incident.

He was just driving away." For some reason I didn't want to tell Barney about the altercation/conversation between Jaynes and the two cops afterward.

"So there wasn't any collusion between the cops and Jaynes?"

"I'm not sure what you're getting at. Is—"

"You haven't been around Farmington for a while, have you? Did you ever hear about what Jaynes did?"

"Well, I talked a little with him about it in the restaurant. He said, in a sort of elliptical way, that he had shot a young Navajo boy who worked for him and went to prison for five years for it."

"Uh huh. Did he mention why he did it?"

"He said the kid had been stealing from him and that the kid was going to spread some lies, some damaging lies, about him and that it was more of a case of self-defense."

"Yeah, that's what was argued in his trial, and except for the self-defense part, that was what the prosecution went with. Because the boy was shot in the back at a distance of about fifteen feet, the self-defense argument didn't hold up and Jaynes was found guilty of manslaughter. He got ten years."

"And got out in five." I was wondering where Barney was going.

"Well, there's a different story about the case. I was working with the D.A.'s office back in 1983 when the trial took place and we all knew that the stealing story was a crock. What happened was that Jaynes was dealing coke and heroin out of the mortuary and the kid was his runner. Maybe the boy was going to rat, maybe he had ripped Jaynes off, we never knew for sure, but we were convinced that dope was the reason for the murder. But the D.A. knew the manslaughter charge was a slam-dunk so he left all of the drug stuff out of the trial, figuring it would muddy the issue."

"No shit?" I was surprised at these revelations, even though I had no problem believing that Jaynes was into hard stuff. What else was there to do in a place like Shiprock?

"Yes, shit. A lot of the guys at the D.A.'s office are pissed off he got out so quick. And then went right back to work at the mortuary. There's no way he would be back in the dope business now, with a parole officer visiting him every week, but there's some animosity towards him.

"But here's the thing. There were two police officers whose names were mentioned in the heroin/coke scene. They didn't get charged with anything, maybe because of judicial influence, but their hands looked a little dirty. One of them was kicked up to detective and the other was demoted to traffic."

"Smuff and Miller."

"Right."

I must have looked at him blankly, because that was the state of my mind. All of the threads and tendrils had tied themselves into a big blankness.

"So let's go fight for Truth, Justice and the American Way," the burly barrister bellowed, and we walked down to his Jaguar XKE. At least we'd be wooing Lady Justice in style.

We got to the Courthouse with five minutes to spare and took our places in the back of the room. Barney immediately started talking to some lawyers and court officials near the judge's bench and it was obvious it was not about my parking ticket.

I took out the David Dodge book, a Dell mapback, and continued my reading from the night before, and it was ten minutes later that I heard the bailiff announce in a stentorian voice, "All rise for the honorable Judge Lawrence T. Slinger!"

The judge was in his fifties, with sleek silver hair parted on the side and flowing over his ears senatorially. His flowing black robes valiantly tried to disguise his corpulence, and failed miserably. He strode to the bench and sat behind it as we all sat down after him.

"Okay, let's get this traffic court going. First case."

One of the under-assistant D.A.s at the prosecution table called out a name and I was back to David Dodge. Thirty minutes later, Barney Eastwick sat down beside me and said, "We're up next. I guess I don't need to tell you to let me do the talking."

"My life is in your hands, brother."

"And would I let my broth—"

Barney's filial pronouncement was interrupted by the braying of the bailiff: "Knees Calhoon! Improper parking!"

My trial had begun.

At this point in the narrative, Erle Stanley Gardner would have dictated a scintillating, and 90% plausible, courtroom dialogue, with strident objections and Masonesque histrionics. All I can do is tell what happened.

Barney and I stood while the sub-deputy D.A. read out the charge. When he said "tires were 20.5 inches from the curb," I saw the judge's face grow a shade redder and his jaw tighten. As soon as the last word of the charge was read, he turned to me and scoffed, "You are challenging the measuring abilities of our fine police force, Mr. Calhoon?"

I started to open my mouth to say any number of wrong things when Barney quickly jumped in. "Your honor, we stipulate to the simple facts of the case. Our objection is to the way the law is worded—and enforced—which we argue is antithetical to its intended purpose: to make the streets safer."

"Do tell. Well, let's hear what the prosecution has to say and we'll get to your argument."

The sub-deputy re-stated the case by pretty much re-reading the charge. Tires were 20.5 inches away when they should have been 18 or less. "Call Patrolman Molly Miller."

The meter maid/officer was dressed as nattily as she had been yesterday as she pushed through the doors across from the jury box, which was empty. She sat in the witness box and took the oath. Detective Smuff entered at the same time and sat near the back of the courtroom.

The sub-deputy spoke from his desk. "You are a police traffic officer named Molly Miller?"

"Yes, I am."

"You saw a car parked too far from the curb and gave it a ticket, after measuring the distance from the curb to the near tire as being 20.5 inches, did you not?"

"I did."

"Was the car the property of Knees Calhoon, the defendant?"

"It was."

"Your witness."

Barney stood up and smiled at the empty jury box. Then he turned to Miller and said, "Thank you, Officer Miller, for your excellent testimony, all seven words of it. Now, did you notice a vehicle parked in front of the defendant's car?"

"I did."

"Uh, what kind of car was it?"

"It was a Dodge Econoline hearse."

"Big vehicle?"

"Yes."

"Bigger than the defendant's car, which was a—" he looked at me and I mouthed, "Volkswagon Square-back." "Volkswagon Squareback?" he continued in the same tone of voice.

"Yes, bigger."

"So big that it stuck out into traffic even more than the defendant's Squareback?"

"I believe it extended further into the street than did the, uh, defendant's car."

"It was a hearse you say?"

"Yes, from Jaynes' Mortuary in Shiprock."

I was marveling at this slow, deliberate sashay of Lady Justice when the officer's response jerked the judge into action. He sat upright and glared at Barney. "Where are you going with this, Mr. Eastwick? What is the relevance of the type of car that was parked in front of the defendant's?"

"No relevance at all. The only reason I brought up the other vehicle is to show that even though it was in compliance of the law, and my client's not, the complying car was the more dangerously parked. The law needs to be changed to make compliance with it compatible with safety, rather than danger. In other words, since the reason for the law is to ensure that cars don't stick out too far into traffic, the law should address the far side of the car, and not the near side."

Molly Miller sputtered from the witness box, "But Judge, even if we were to start measuring how far it was to the far side of the car, we don't know what that figure is. We'd have to stop giving tickets for this until they decided what that figure should be."

Barney Eastwick suggested, "Maybe you could ask the city department that paints the white lines that define each parking space?"

"But it's so much easier just to measure to the near wheels!" Molly whined.

"This whole case is ridiculous," the judge boomed. "How much is the fine for this thing?"

"Uh, ten dollars, your honor," the sub-deputy announced.

Judge Slinger turned his hefty body to face me. "*Mis*ter Calhoon. You don't live in Farmington, do you." He said it as a statement.

"No, I don't, your honor."

"You stayin' long?"

"Not any longer than I have to, your honor."

"Well, I'm inclined to instruct the D.A.'s office to drop the charges in hopes that we will soon see the backside of you as you skedaddle home. Is that satisfactory?"

Again my mouth opened to say something inadvisable when Barney interjected, "One hundred percent satisfactory, your honor. And I'm sure the proper department of the local government will look into revising the laws concerning how parking parameters are measured."

The judge, Molly and the sub-deputy glared at Barney for a few seconds then glared at each other in an oddly chicken-like sequence where none of them glared at the one glaring at him.

Finally, the sub-deputy intoned, "The prosecution withdraws the charges."

Barney and I smiled at each other and left the courtroom before I could be told to get out of town again. We drove back to his office, cackling like hens in the XKE, and when we arrived it was just past two p.m.

"Thanks for giving me an opportunity to piss off some well-deserving cops," Barney was saying as we entered the office building. "Especially Miller. Too bad Detective Smuff didn't get called. He tends to sweat noticeably when grilled. The juries eat it up."

"I noticed you playing to the non-existent jury today. What's with that?"

"Just a habit. But a judge is just like a small jury. Say, did you think Judge Slinger was taking this whole case a little too seriously?"

"Well, I don't really know him. I thought *you* did."

"Oh I know him all right. He's been an ass ever since he got demoted to traffic court about seven years ago. But this was somethin' different. It's like he had somethin' personal to pick with you. He coulda made you pay the $10, easy, but it's like he wanted you to just leave."

"It seemed that way to me too."

By this time we were in his office relaxing. I piped up, "Well, Barney, there went two hours of your billable time. How much you need for your pound of flesh?"

"The same as for your divorce."

I nodded. A quart of Jim Beam and a quart of the store's second best tequila. I'd have to take care of that tomorrow—for the rest of today I had plans that were crawling around in my head like worms in an ant farm.

I said goodbye to Barney and drove back to the Arrowhead. I took a shower and smoked a joint while a movie with Alan Ladd and Sophia Loren played on the silent TV. Great wet pearl-diving blouse scene.

By five p.m. I was hungry and it was time to put my plan in action. This time I wasn't going to leave town with Billy lying dead on the bluffs.

CHAPTER FIVE: Snakes on a Plain

I knew I had plenty of time to kill so I started out heading east to see what sort of restaurants there were towards Aztec. I spotted a likely looking one, La Fiesta, and had a superb combo plate with sopaipillas and honey *during* the meal. A half hour later I was driving out of town to the west, towards Shiprock.

This was a part of town I hadn't revisited and it really took me back. I passed the intersection where Apache Street, a major east-west residential thoroughfare hit Main Street and then passed where the La Plata highway headed off to the north to Mancos. Immediately ahead of me was the two-mile long Harper's Hill, a 15% grade that led up to the plateau around Kirtland. I saw off to my left the San Juan River valley and beyond that the western reach of the Bluffs. It was really a beautiful valley, especially out here where the farms were small and well-manicured. I noticed that the highway department had put in a run-off lane for trucks coming down the hill. If their brakes failed they could veer off onto the run-off and be slowed by about fifty yards of level sand. Good idea. Harper's Hill was notoriously dangerous back in the 50s and 60s because of its steepness and length, and the four-lane divided highway they'd put in hadn't made it any safer if your brakes went out.

As I chugged up the hill in my Squareback, gray-blue, the same kind of car Harrison Ford drove in his Amish detective movie, I saw off to my right a cliff of rugged sandstone that ended only as I topped the rise. The highway divided the top of the mesa in a straight line—heading directly into the sun.

Why do I always seem to be driving west when the sun is going down?

I was just getting to the turn-off to Kirtland, about ten miles from Farmington, when I saw ahead a road that led off to the right to the El Paso Natural Gas golf course. That really brought back some memories. Billy and I and some friends used to play golf there almost every day for a couple of summers back in '65 and '66, when I was just out of high school. It was for El Paso workers and their dependents only, but since we always had Ron Oliverri around, whose father and uncle were surveyors for EP, we had no problems playing nine holes a day. There was usually no one around to care, anyway. It was just a nine-hole golf course—no pro shop or anything.

I decided to see what it looked like today and turned off on a well-traveled dirt road. It angled to the left and over a small hill and there it was—almost exactly the way I had last seen it.

The fairways were a water-deprived green and the roughs were sandy dunes, completely covered with sagebrush, cactus, and species of stickers that probably plagued the dinosaurs. Even if you saw exactly where you duffed the ball out into the rough, there was a good chance you couldn't get to it without placing your shins in serious jeopardy. There was a lake hole and if it hadn't been for periodic night excursions where we'd wade the lake shoeless, picking up balls with our toes, we'd have never been able to afford to play the course, even though it was free. It was damned easy to lose balls in the rough out here.

I parked the car at a little shed that stood next to the tee for Hole #1 and walked over to the only bench on the whole nine holes. I sat and looked out over fairway #1 and fairway #9 beyond it, my back to the desert.

The first inkling of twilight was on me and I fished out a joint and lit it. An empty golf course is a beautiful sight at the end of the day. It was a day like this that

Billy and I found my old pet Mojina, a five-foot garden snake on one of the middle holes by the lake. It was out in the rough and my ball practically hit it. We took the snake with us and kept it at my apartment where I lived the summer of '65. Billy was still in high school and was living at home with our mother. I moved out of the house the day I graduated from high school. In those days practically everybody did. Nowadays they've made things so rough on 18-year-old people that they're forced to be wards of their parents up into their 20s. It used to be that only rich assholes went to college paid for by their daddies. Regular people worked their way through or went into the service and got the GI bill. But then they raised tuitions so much that it stopped being men and women who went to college and started being children. So of course mommy and daddy freaked out when little Susie and Johnny started taking drugs and having sex. Hell, what did they think college was for?

There's no telling how far my internal diatribe would have gone on if I hadn't heard an ominous rustling in the sage behind me.

I jumped up and saw the stickers move a bit about five feet away. "Holy shit!" I exclaimed as I saw some other stickers move about four feet away from that. I was being snuck up upon! Then I saw the snake.

It was not as long and fat as Mojina, whom I returned to the rough at this course when I left Farmington for the army in 1967, but it was just as beautiful. It was relaxing in the evening air, which was getting cooler as the fall came on. It had the markings of a rattler, but much more subdued. I knew nothing about snakes, but I had been told back in 1965 that it was a garden snake and I'm sticking to that.

The plan I had roiling around in my mind involved revenge, and all of these things blended together to remind me of something Billy had told me in the early 80s, about Marty Jaynes. Billy knew Marty pretty well and when the Jaynes Mortuary opened up in Shiprock in 1980 Billy went out to see the place a couple of times. The way Billy told it to me was that it was maybe Billy's first visit and there was nobody around the place, just Marty and Billy. Marty was down in the morgue doing something and Billy was looking around the upstairs where the caskets were on display. No bodies, just empty, open caskets. Billy was checking out an especially frilly casket when he saw something that made him shout out for Marty to come check it out.

Marty came up the stairs and looked into the casket where Billy pointed. Marty jumped and shouted and looked around quickly. Seeing all of the doors closed and no one in sight, he reached in and pulled out a two-foot long snake, who knows what kind. Not a rattler, obviously. Marty took the snake and went out the back door and came back a few minutes later. He had told Billy that to the Navajos a snake is a very powerful being that must be respected for many things—and blamed for many others. But the last thing you want associated with a member of your clan's death is a snake. As Marty had put it to Billy, "If any customer had ever seen a snake in any of my caskets, or even in my building anywhere, he'd have been my last Navajo customer. He'd'a told all his clansmen and they'd'a told all their wives and before long the mortuary would have been taboo."

The snake had moved only a foot or so since this memory had hit me and I started thinking that maybe I could use him for my plan. It was a half-baked plan anyway and everyone knows that snakes make everything more fun.

So I ran over to my car to see what I could use to hold the snake. In the back—a Squareback is essentially a station wagon—there was a cardboard box that had some books in it. Plus a bunch of Styrofoam packing popcorn. I took the books out and brought the box to where I had seen the snake. It was still there and I could see it well, even though it was rapidly getting dark. I picked up the snake and put it in the box with the popcorn and closed the four flaps inside each other. It didn't seem to mind.

I had no idea of what I would do with the snake. I'd figure that out when I got to the mortuary. It was going to be 10:30 at night and some shady people I didn't like were going to meet at a mortuary in Shiprock New Mexico at the end of a dead end road. And I was going to spy on them with a snake as my partner.

This wasn't much of a plan, but it sounded like it was going to be fun.

But then came the final nail in the coffin of my strategy. As I walked in the dusk with a box full of four-foot snake in my hands, I stepped on something. And it turned out to be a two-foot snake. I put it in the box with the four-footer. Why the hell not?

CHAPTER SIX: Stakeout

The rest of the trip to Shiprock was about like I remembered it was back when my family knew some people who worked at the helium plant and we used to visit them regularly. It's a pleasant road and there used to be a stretch where the cottonwoods were planted in rows alongside the road and their branches met overhead, like something you'd expect to see on the Natchez Trace. Those trees were no longer there.

As I approached Shiprock from the east I could see the monument off in the distance to the southwest. It was so big that it looked a lot nearer than it was. If you've seen any old western movie you've probably seen the tall, jagged Shiprock, which is the remnant of an antediluvian volcano. The cone has completely worn away leaving only the magma, extending almost 1800 feet above the desert in the vague shape of a clipper ship. Billy and I had driven up to it a couple of times and touched it, both times getting run off by the Navajo Police. People have tried to climb it and some have died trying.

I almost passed the place I was looking for, a little café with the quaint name of Chat & Chew. I wasn't interested in chatting, but I had some time to kill and I'd always heard there was some good chew at the Chat & Chew in Shiprock.

I pulled into the parking lot at the Chat & Chew at ten till eight. I ordered a burger with green chile and onions and thousand island dressing with French fries and cole slaw and pulled out my David Dodge and settled into the booth for a while. The cover of the book was fantastic, with a red-robed Death rowing a floating coffin with a huge, ten-foot "cigarette" as cargo. It looked like they used to roll their joints more professionally back in the 50s than I do now. The smoke of the cigarette wafted into the dark sky in the form of a buxom and naked bighaired babe. The rear cover of the book was a mapback, with a double map showing the California coastline around San Francisco and Monterey and Carmel in the top map, and the northern half of San Francisco in the bottom map. The banner above the maps emblazoned "Where marijuana and murder make a thrilling story". My kinda book.

An hour and a half later it was getting close to the Chat & Chew's closing hour of ten. I was just finishing the book when the lady behind the counter started looking at me as if she'd like for me to go. I read the last page and left, leaving a big tip and telling her it was the best burger I'd had in a long time. It was.

I got in the Squareback and wondered if I knew how to get to Jaynes' Mortuary. I had a vague idea of where it was but had never been there. I didn't want to ask anyone, just in case. . .

I knew it was at the end of a dead end road and I was pretty sure it was on the southern edge of town off of Highway 666 that led down to Window Rock and Gallup. Down in Jim Chee country, where Hillerman says he has a trailer down by the river. I headed west and turned south on 666. There was a fast food place at the intersection that I remembered had the best Navajo tacos. Damn. Maybe I should have eaten there.

I decided to just drive around the area on the side streets. Sooner or later I was bound to see a Dead End sign. According to the hearse, the mortuary was at the end of the road. I'd just go down any dead end roads I saw. It was five after ten.

It took me five minutes of driving before I saw it. I actually saw the red neon glowing down a dark, dark road before I saw the sign that said "DEAD END". I turned onto the road and saw that it was two blocks long, with the mortuary straddling the end of the road. There were about four houses on the two blocks but none of them were near the road. They were all set back about twenty feet and were hidden by trees. We must not be far from the San Juan River.

It was coal dark and the moon wasn't out, which was good, because there wasn't any place to hide my car. My best bet to stake out the place was to park off the road about a half block from the mortuary and hope the person who owned the property didn't see me. Chances were good that anyone driving up the road to the mortuary wouldn't see my car unless they veered right at me.

I found a good spot and shut off my engine. I had turned my lights off when I entered the road. Now came the stakeout. I was close enough to see that there weren't any cars parked in the parking lot in front of the building and it didn't look like there were any roads around the building.

The only lights besides the neon sign were in a small window on the left side of the main floor. The mortuary was a two-story affair, but the bottom floor was a basement, half sunk into the earth, and the top floor was just up a few steps from the parking lot. From what Billy had said, the morgue was in the basement and the top floor was the part the public would see.

It was not quite 10:15 so I figured I might as well see if I could put the snakes to a good use. I got out of the car—after first turning off the dome light—and took the box, from which came a rustling sound that sent a chill down my spine. I wasn't exactly sure of what I was going to do—I just thought that sabotaging the mortuary was a good idea.

I headed for the south end of the building, where the light was. It looked like a bathroom light that had been left on; or maybe an office light. It was up about eight feet off the ground. I went up to it and saw that it was tightly closed and didn't look like anything I could jimmy open. My eyes were getting used to the dark and I could see some other windows, some on the bottom floor right above ground level, but they were all closed, too. So much for my idea of mortuary sabotage. It was a stupid idea, anyway.

So I went back to the car and put the box in the back, checking to make sure that the folded flaps were still tightly closed. I didn't want to come out to the car and find one or more of the snakes missing.

I sat in the dark, listening to the occasional rustle of the box, and had a smoke while waiting. A few minutes later I saw the lights of a truck that turned onto the dead end street and passed by me. It pulled in front of the mortuary and parked and two large men got out. They leaned up against the side of the truck, lit cigarettes and mumbled a few words I couldn't pick up. They sounded like Navajos.

A few minutes later another set of lights came up the street and I saw that it was the Jaynes Mortuary hearse. Jaynes got out and said something to the two men and they entered the building.

Was there any more? What about Miller and Smuff?

Not more than two minutes after the trio had entered the building another car came and parked, a Cadillac de Ville. Out of it lumbered a very large man. Slinger! What role did he have in this caper? And more importantly, was there really a caper?

Slinger strode into the building and I hunkered down in the car. What about Miller and Smuff? Weren't they supposed to be here for this meeting or whatever it was?

I had to piss. Why didn't I do it at the Chat & Chew? In the noir books the dicks always talked about the bottles they brought along on stakeouts. But they lived in big cities like Frisco or Miami. Hell, I was in Shiprock New Mexico. It was better than being at

Bohemian Grove with Greenspan and Kissinger and that crowd. I could piss on any tree I wanted.

I got out of the car and was relaxing the bladder against a small cottonwood when I heard a female voice chortle, "That looks like some kind of violation, doesn't it, Wally?" Uh oh.

CHAPTER SEVEN: Introduction to a Trocar

Patrolman Molly Miller had her service revolver out and pointed in my direction. Detective Smuff lit a cigarette and sneered, leaning up against the Squareback. "Looks like parking up the road and scouting the area was a good idea, Molly."

"I get 'em every once in a while, Wally," she said huskily and after I zipped up, pushed me to the car. "Let's go tell it to the judge."

The three of us walked to the door of the mortuary and entered. I wasn't holding my hands in the air but Miller kept the gun in her hand. They acted like they knew I didn't have any sort of weapon. They were right. I wasn't even sure if I had a brain any longer. What a plan!

The front room of the mortuary was large and full of open caskets. I didn't look to see if there were any bodies in them—humans *or* snakes. There was a staircase heading down towards the back of the room and we walked to it and descended ten steps to a dank, musty room that looked like the lab of a mad scientist. Judge Slinger and Marty Jaynes were talking next to a flat, metal table with grooves running down each side of it into a trough-like container. On the tables was a sheet-covered, man-sized object that I assumed was a corpse. If P.D. James were telling this you'd get a detailed description of every item in the room, but I'm doing it, and you'll have to use your imagination. It was a morgue, for pete's sake. I didn't *want* to know what was in it.

Slinger and Jaynes looked surprised to see me. The two Navajos, huge men who looked like brothers, stood on the other side of the table and looked bored. I figured them for the muscle of the gang.

"What the hell is *he* doing here?" Slinger sputtered, his enormous belly draping over the table and jiggling.

"Ask him," Smuff said, smirking.

I had no idea what I was going to say, but Slinger didn't look at me. He turned to Smuff and muttered, "Make sure the Etcitty boys keep an eye on him." Smuff said something in Navajo and the two brothers nodded, but didn't look at me.

Jaynes spouted, "Well, I'll ask him! What the hell are you doin' here, Calhoon?"

"I came out to see that thing you were talking about at the Avery. That tro-something."

"The trocar? It's kinda late to be getting' curious about undertakin'.

The judge waddled away from the table a couple of steps and said, "Miller, go check his car. Smuff, what does he know about us?"

Miller left and before Smuff could answer, Jaynes broke in, "Smuff doesn't know any more than what I told him when I called him to come and ticket Calhoon's car. Look, nothing has happened since this afternoon when you left him off of the ticket. Other than him comin' out here and snoopin' around."

"That's what worries me. You told me if I let him off he'd leave town."

"Hey," I complained, "I'm right here. You can talk to me." I immediately regretted it because I wasn't sure what I was going to say.

Finally the judge looked at me and with narrowed eyes asked, "So what do you know about what happened here in 1983?"

The question surprised me and I mumbled, "Uh, you mean when Jaynes killed that Navajo kid?"

"Yes."

I wondered how much to tell. "Well, Jaynes said he shot the kid for stealing. I figured there was something more than that but, hell, it's no business of mine."

"What do you mean, 'more than that'?"

"Hey look, I'm a man of the world. I don't care if people use, sell or worship drugs. I've been known to take a puff or two myself."

The judge and Smuff snorted. Jaynes looked a little worried. He started to say something but the judge cut him off. "Drugs. That's what you think is going on?"

"I don't think anything is going on. I came out to see a trocar."

Jaynes' face lit up and he quickly said, "That's right. The trocar. Here lemme show you one." He walked to a table and picked up a metal instrument in the shape of a hollow cylinder, about a foot in length and a half-inch in diameter. It was beveled and sharp on one end. He brought it over to me and pointed it at my midsection.

The judge looked on thoughtfully as Jaynes continued. "Y'see. We gotta drain all the insides out of a body and so we insert this thing in several places in the abdomen and. . ." He tried to look maniacal and went on, "So what do you think, Calhoon? What do you think of the trocar now?"

"Other than being an anagram of 'carrot', not much," I countered and the Etcittys snickered but still didn't look at me.

Smuff saw the consternation on Jaynes' face and walked over to another table and picked up an instrument that looked like the trocar in Jaynes' hand, but at least four times as large, with a diameter of about 2 inches. "How about this baby, Calhoon? Ya' got an anagram for this thing?"

Jaynes sputtered, "That's a horse trocar, Smuff."

"Okay. Okay," I stammered. "I get the point. I'm not supposed to be here. I haven't seen anything and I'm on my way out of town."

"But I don't believe you, Mr. Calhoon," the judge said, wheezing. "I think you are here because you know there's more than drugs involved. I think you're here, perhaps at the instigation of that shyster Eastwick, to spy on us for our other activities."

I didn't know exactly where he was going but I tried to put a knowing look on my face, hoping he might continue and actually tell me what was going on.

"You tolerant types make me ill, Calhoon. You have no qualms about illegal substances but as soon as a man takes a small advantage of a person who has since left this plane of existence, using only the physical shell that the person has left behind for his modest pleasure, you become a moralist. You have no perspective. You—"

I was just beginning to digest what the judge was saying—and it wasn't sitting well—when Molly Miller's legs appeared in the stairway leading up to the top floor. She entered the room and I saw that she was carrying the cardboard box. Still closed.

The judge continued, "We are but a group of simple souls with a taste for life that so many ignorant people consider, shall we say, perverse?"

I was hardly listening to the madman because I was intent on Miller's actions. She walked over and placed the box on the table next to what I assumed was the corpse's head.

"All he had in the car was this box. And a roach in the ashtray. Looked like crummy Mexican weed."

"Here. Lemme see what you got," Smuff said and, after placing the horse trocar on the operating table, flipped open the four flaps of the box to reveal a level sea of white Styrofoam popcorn. All of the people in the room: me, Judge Slinger, Marty Jaynes, Detective Smuff, Molly Miller and even the Etcitty brothers leaned a little closer to the box to see.

Detective Smuff grunted and reached his right hand into the pile of Styrofoam. A look of recognition flitted across his face and he suddenly gave a yell that startled us all. He whipped his hand out of the box and on the end of his forefinger was the head of a writhing, two-foot snake. Its body slapped against the face of one of the Etcittys and the Navajo let out a howl that drowned out the cursing of Smuff. Everyone jumped back and I thought, "There's only two ways you can stick a finger into a snake and I'm glad he picked that one." I reached out and pushed the box off the table onto the floor and the other snake, the four-foot one, fell out of the popcorn and curled around the other Etcitty's leg.

As the scream of the second terrified Navajo pierced through the chaos, everyone froze—except me. The trocar in Jaynes' hand was pointing at the ground and before anyone knew it I was running up the stairs.

I slammed through the door to the cool New Mexico night and ran to my car. I could hear shouts from inside the mortuary but so far no one had come out of the place. I started it up and peeled out, making a quick 90 degree turn and was headed out of the dead end street when I saw two figures run out of the building in the rear-view mirror. Miller and Smuff it looked like.

I screeched around the corner and soon found myself on Highway 64 speeding through the sleepy town of Shiprock on my way back to Farmington.

CHAPTER EIGHT: The Flight of the Squareback

I had about a half mile lead on the cop car as I left Shiprock and I kept the VW at 80, which was about its maximum speed. They could have caught me within a few miles but they seemed to be biding their time. They didn't have their flashing lights on but stayed about ten car lengths back as I passed Kirtland a few minutes later.

I didn't have time to be thinking but I couldn't help but wonder what the judge was talking about. Necrophilia? Was he saying that they had a necrophilia ring out at the Jaynes Mortuary? And that maybe *that* was the reason for the murder of Sammy Arthur? That would explain their trying to kill me for simply parking my car outside the mortuary. They knew I wasn't going to turn anyone in for dealing coke or heroin, but who knows how I'd react to necrophilia?

Hell, I didn't even know how I'd react. It does seem like the ultimate victimless crime. . .

The terror and chaos of the scene I'd just gone through in the basement of the mortuary was jangling through my mind as I kept the Squareback floorboarded through the dense black night. *Terror. Chaos. Horse trocar*. Goddammit! Why do I always come up with the perfect comeback about ten minutes too late!

I was driving like a madman and coming up on Harper's Hill. I'd have to slow down for the long, steep decline. I had just tapped the brake when the lights behind me loomed much closer, then almost touched my car. They were going to ram me as I was heading down Harper's Hill and run me off the road. How could I stop them from doing just that?

We were halfway down the hill and they had just bumped me, making me accelerate a bit to a speed way too fast for going down the most dangerous hill in the Four Corners area. I was going to crash!

And then, out of the corner of my eye, I saw the truck run-off ramp to the right. Without thinking I yanked the wheel to the right and bowled off the highway into a long stretch of deep sand that slowed me down so fast I banged my face against the wheel. In the rear mirror on the driver's side of my car I saw the two in the cop car behind me, startled by my quick action, start to follow me onto the ramp but they seemed to realize that they'd ram me too hard for *their* safety and tried to continue down Harper's Hill.

They didn't make it. The cop car hit the edge of the road at a 45 degree angle and flipped. I couldn't see it after the first flip but it sounded like it kept flipping all the way down the hill. I was pretty sure I didn't have to worry about those two cops any more.

But could I get out of the sand? The car had died so I started it and tried to back up the ramp through the sand. The ramp was just about level where I was stuck in it and with just a bit of maneuvering I was able to pull the car back up onto the highway and continue down Harper's Hill. I saw the cop car, totally demolished, in a ravine off the right side of the road. It was upside down and there was no way I was going to stop and see what the story was.

I had almost made it down the hill when I saw another set of carlights behind me roaring down the hill. It was the Jaynes' Mortuary hearse.

It was hitting about fifty and I had to make a quick decision: should I try to make it to Farmington and see how my story stood up against the mortician's and the judge's? Or should I do something else?

I was at the turnoff to the La Plata highway and took it, making a big sweeping left turn and heading north. Could my Squareback outrun the hearse? I was going to find out. I kicked it back up to 80 and was staying about 100 yards ahead of the hearse when I saw a big sign ahead saying "Glade Hill Road, 1 mile". It gave me an idea.

The hearse was still on my tail when I got to the junction. I turned right and was on the old road I knew so well that would take me to Chokecherry Canyon. I was surprised to see that instead of being the dirt road it used to be, it was now nicely paved and according to the signs would take me to Sunset Avenue, up by the high school! What the—? I didn't know the Glade Road connected to Sunset. Must be new.

But I saw the dirt road that led to Chokecherry Canyon heading off to the left off the paved highway and took it. If I had to make my stand, I was going to do it on my turf, and thanks to Billy's and my exploration days, I considered Chokecherry Canyon my turf.

The hearse followed me onto the dirt road, about 200 yards back.

CHAPTER NINE: Chokecherry Canyon

The canyon where the highschoolers had their keg parties was about two miles up the dirt road and I still had a lead on the hearse when I reached it and drove right next to the campfire site and stopped. There was no moon and it was almost pitch black but I knew the area well. I got out of the car and ran across the sooty ground to the edge of the 30-foot high sandstone rock formation. The hearse pulled next to my VW and I heard both doors open. By the dome light I could see that it was Jaynes and Judge Slinger who got out. It looked like the judge had a gun in his hand.

I was thinking that in this darkness there's no way they could see me crouched up against the rock when I saw a flashlight flicker on in Jaynes' hand. Damn! The light angled towards me and I ran farther down the edge of the sandstone and ducked into the crevice that we called Fat Man's Misery. They must have seen me just before I ducked in because I heard Jaynes give a shout and the light settled on the opening of the hole in the cliffside. I knew Fat Man's Misery well and climbed a little farther into it.

The hole in the rock was about the height of a man and it led into a small antechamber that was big enough for two or three people. But as you moved farther the only direction was up. If it had been daylight I could have seen, 25 feet above me, daylight through the opening in the mesa-top. But even though it was pitch dark I was able to climb to a position about fifteen feet above ground level where the internal opening was barely big enough for my torso.

Jaynes made it to the entrance to Fat Man's Misery first and shone his light up into it, revealing my feet on a shelf. Then I heard a wheezing Judge Slinger join him. I moved a few feet higher and the light was no longer on my feet.

"Come on out, Calhoon," I heard Jaynes yell and I kept quiet.

"It'll be easier for all of us if you come down now," the judge added, breathing as if he was on his deathbed.

"There's no way you'll let me walk, knowing all I know," I shouted down the tunnel, thinking that I didn't really know all that much. But they thought I did, I guess.

"What *do* you know?" the judge asked. "Maybe I should tell you everything and then I'll really have a good reason for killing you."

I didn't say anything and then I heard Jaynes stutter, "W-w-what do you mean, 'everything'?"

Slinger ignored him and spoke to me. "You don't think that the story ends with drugs and our little, uh, peccadillo, do you? You think *that* would make me want you to get out of town and never come back? I know who you are and I know what you're after." The judge was shouting into the opening of Fat Man's Misery standing next to Jaynes with the flashlight.

I was ready to ask, "What do you mean?" when I heard Jaynes ask, "What do you mean?"

"Get with the program, Marty, you know what I'm talking about. I'm talking about Calhoon's brother. He was the most beautiful specimen of manflesh I ever saw. I knew I had to have him and I would have too, sooner or later."

"Whaaaat?" Jaynes moaned and the flashlight veered away. "You—and Billy? My best friend?"

"Get real, you little pissant. What do you think turned me away from the living for my needs? The disappointment of not having what I craved more than anything else in the world—"

"You sonofabitch!" I heard the thunk of something metallic hitting against something fleshy and then the gun went off. Three times. The light went out.

I was sweating profusely even though it was a cool night. I waited on my perch inside Fat Man's Misery my mind roiling about these revelations, revelations that I may have suspected, but never knew enough about. Then I heard a huffing from directly inside the tunnel below. The flashlight stayed off.

"I can't see you, but I don't think I need to see you," came the puffing voice of Judge Slinger. He was entering the crevice.

I scuttled up a few more steps, trying to keep to the left where I would be hidden by a slight curve from the vestibule below. A shot rang out and I felt something hot whiz past my face and exit the opening at the top of Fat Man's Misery.

"Are you saying you killed my brother?" I yelled down the shaft, trying to buy some time.

"You know I did," came the wheezing reply from below. "You knew all along, didn't you? That's why you came back to town, isn't it?"

I was slowly moving farther up the tunnel, trying to be quiet about it. I didn't want to give my position away but I had to find out more. "But why?"

"I wanted him but he acted as if he didn't know I did. I used to see him around town and at the mortuary and he simply refused to understand my wants and needs. So I told him that there was a guy up at the Bolack well up on the Bisti that wanted him for a job and drove him up there. I had to kill him; he was driving me crazy."

I could hear him moving around, trying to find a good angle to fire at me once again and I moved several more feet up the shaft, almost to the top. He fired again and this time the bullet missed me by a couple of feet. I quietly slid over the top of the opening atop the mesa and poked my head down and yelled, "I'm stuck, judge, either shoot me or come and get me. I'm at the end of the tunnel." I was hoping that Judge Slinger didn't know anything about Fat

Man's Misery.

I figured he only had one bullet left and wanted to make it a good one, and sure enough, I heard him climb up a few feet, trying to get past the curve that kept him from shooting me directly. I had him!

The reason they call the cave Fat Man's Misery is that it's pretty narrow about halfway up the 25-foot shaft. Too narrow for anyone any larger than my 180 pounds. But the miserable part of the shaft is that once you get about ten feet up the thing, it's almost impossible to get back down, not without falling the ten feet onto some really jagged rocks. Anyone of any heft would break both legs and a back trying to jump down.

The only way out—is up. And it's not for a Fat Man.

I stood up on top of the mesa and started trotting to the south along the top of the cliff. I had done this enough with Billy when we were teenagers to know where to step, even in the dark. Five minutes later I was back down to road level and five minutes after that I was back at my car. I could hear the judge yelling inside Fat Man's Misery.

I figured if I waited long enough I would hear the sound of the sixth bullet, but I didn't wait. I drove back down the dirt road and left onto the Glade Road heading to Sunset Avenue. If the bullet didn't end his misery, the varmints would. But then, maybe there would be a high school beer bust this weekend and the judge and the hearse would be found. And Jaynes' body, which I assumed was up by the entrance to the cave.

I didn't care. I drove through town to the Arrowhead Motel, picked up my suitcase and stuff and headed towards Bloomfield. I had three joints to get me to Las Cruces and the relative sanity of the bars. That ought to about do it.

On the way home I thought about Billy. I wasn't coming back to Farmington.

THE BEST REVENGE

A SORT-OF WESTERN

The young man's eyes opened and beheld ten thousand stars. The Colorado night air was cold but under the blanket he had bought from Jimmie Yazzie years back he was comfortable. Nothing had awakened him, but he was wide awake and he knew he wanted to get started, even though daylight was a couple of hours away.

He stood up and rolled the gray and black Navajo blanket into a tight cylinder and cinched it with a couple of leather strips. He had slept fully clothed—except for his boots—and thought about how good a bath would feel. Maybe this was the day he'd have one. The campfire was still glowing and he threw on a few sticks for his coffee.

Hosteen, tethered a few feet away, snorted and acted as if he was ready to get on with their journey too, even though he was undoubtedly hungry. All either of them had the day before were some apples because they had skirted Cañon City and the provisions were running very low. Hosteen, a tall sorrel obtained from Henry Begay two years ago, was a magnificent horse and had made the two-week journey fully packed without complaint. There were roads all the way from Farmington, in New Mexico, to their destination, but the two travelers had mainly kept off them, paralleling them a few miles to the east where the land was a bit less mountainous, and the dangers of meeting curious or malevolent miners less probable.

The young man pulled on his boots, sipped his coffee, and had an apple before packing everything onto Hosteen. He was especially careful with the oversized, bulging saddlebags that only a horse the size of Hosteen could have carried. He cleaned up the fire, fed Hosteen a couple of apples and climbed into the saddle and they continued north, with the black Colorado sky dotted with stars above.

It was about an hour later that the young man noticed a faint blue glow on the near horizon ahead and with every step a hundred stars died out. They were approaching a ridge that the young man sensed was the last one they'd find before they reached their goal. The blue glow was winking out the stars, not the looming sun that would soon strip off the cold, September night. Both the young man and his horse seemed to sense the excitement of journey's end as they approached the crest with the blue glow, which had by now obliterated almost all of the stars to the north.

They reached the top and looked down on the most beautiful thing the young man had ever seen, or imagined.

~ ~ ~ ~

Two weeks earlier, the young man had just picked the last bushel of apples from Henry Begay's tree when he heard the gunshots. He climbed down the ladder and walked with the basket back to his house a hundred yards away just north of the San Juan River. He knew his father didn't like it when the cowboys from Durango got drunk and rode down to Farmington to raise a little hell, and for that reason the young man liked it even less.

"Hey Pa!" he yelled as he dropped the basket on the back porch. He'd take them to Henry's clan, the wolf clan, the next day if he had the chance. They'd probably meet him a mile or so down the road towards Kirtland. "I got Henry's apples."

"I'm out front," Pa said, and the young man walked around the house and sat down on the front steps at the feet of Pa, who was sitting in the rocking chair on the big front porch, smoking his pipe and staring out into the dusk. "Those Durango boys just don't know how to have fun, do they?"

"Aw, don't mind them, Pa. They do whatever they have to do to get the girls. If there was any girls to speak of in Farmington, I might be doing the same thing." The gunshots were coming more often now, and getting a bit closer. Probably near the train tracks on the south side of Farmington. Pa smiled because he knew that there *were* some girls in Farmington, mostly young, timid Mormon girls, and that his son had romanced a few of them in his own way.

Farmington had been an incorporated town for about 20 years and it was mainly inhabited by hardworking farmers, orcharders, tradespeople and most of all, Mormons. It was not an easy life but the land was rich, fueled by three rivers, The Animas, the San Juan and the La Plata. The Navajo name for the area was Totah, which meant "three rivers". The reservation lay to the west and there was a friendly, peaceful relationship between the mystical Indians and the differently mystical Mormons.

Pa and his son were not Mormons, but they respected the townspeople and farmers, who had been here for a couple of generations before Pa migrated to Farmington from Missouri with the young man's mother, who died giving birth to him the year after they arrived.

Durango, fifty miles to the north, in Colorado was a mining town. The people there were rough and rude, but they had to be to scrabble a living from the mountain that was filled with silver and a little gold just south of the town.

The young man was hearing even more shots now. He knew what was going on. The cowboys were drunk and firing their pistols in the air, hoping to impress the young women of Farmington. They rarely did, mainly because the fathers and mothers wouldn't let their daughters out of the houses when there was a wild ride from Durango going on. It happened about once a month, and the cowboys seemed to be satisfied with just annoying the Farmington townspeople for an hour or so before heading back to Durango at a gallop.

He thought he saw some of the cowboys off to the east. It looked like Jerry Jimerfield and his gang. Their reputation preceded them. Calling themselves the "Lords of Durango"—the young man laughed to himself as he thought of that—the gang of Jimerfield, Tommy Beuten, Sid Leavell and Chuck were notorious for their hijinks. Jimerfield was the leader, a tall, gaunt twenty-five-year old who always wore black shirts with a big white hat. He was one of the ugliest men the young man had ever seen with what Doc Smith, the local Farmington druggist/dentist said was a "severe overbite", but there was nobody in Farmington or Durango who got more girls than Jerry Jimerfield. He was the fastest guitar strummer anyone had ever seen and he knew exactly what to say to get almost any girl who got near him to go with him out back of the dance hall for a short, but apparently satisfying good time.

The young man knew them all by reputation, and wished they would get the alcohol out of their systems and get on back to Durango. "Did the new *Scientific American* come in yet, Pa?" he asked and the old man answered, "Not yet."

Pa had raised the young man by himself and had instilled in him an appreciation for reading, especially the magazines that came in about once a month on the train from the east. Pa was the Farmington blacksmith and fix-it man and the young man was going to take over for him someday. But Pa was the real expert on everything he could learn about the world outside New Mexico. He read *Harper's*, *The Strand*, all the way from across the Atlantic with the terrific Sherlock Holmes stories, but his favorite was *Scientific American*. He tinkered with everything he read about in the magazine, using his blacksmith shop to make his own tools and devices. The young man liked all of those magazines too, but he also liked *Deadwood Dick* and *Wild Bill Hickock* stories. In fact, if they didn't spend so much money on the magazines, which were expensively shipped from back east, they'd probably have a lot more money saved.

The gunshots sounded like they were only a couple hundred yards away and the young man saw the Lords of Durango shooting in the air, whooping like wild men, their horses probably drunk too.

"I'll take Henry's apples to him tomorrow, Pa," the young man repeated. Pa had planted one of the finest apple orchards in the county not long after the young man was born and it was the son's job to maintain it. It was almost as lucrative as blacksmithing and their apples were known throughout the town for their succulence. The young man spent part of every day preening the orchard and in the fall, picking the apples that filled the trees.

Most orchards were planted in rows, for maximum efficiency, but Pa had been reading about something called the golden ratio, or the divine proportion, when he did the planting. So their orchard looked haphazard and random seen from the ground, as if planted by a psychotic. But Pa knew that if you could somehow get up above the land—in a balloon, perhaps—you could see the beautiful spiral shape of the orchard, winding like the shell of a sea creature away from a central tree.

Two years back Pa knew that his son needed a good horse and had arranged for Henry Begay, who had an uncle in Window Rock who knew horses, to bring him up a half dozen to choose from. In return, Henry's clan would get the lion's share of the apples from the tree of their choice.

The uncle, William Etcitty, was a medicine man for the clan, and he was stoic when the deal was made at the house. Pa had let his son decide and he picked a small, young sorrel, which he named Hosteen. Everybody knew "Hosteen" meant "friend" and it was a good name for a horse. But how did the young man know that the horse would grow so large and magnificent?

Pa, the young man and William then walked out to the orchard to select a tree. The orchard was large and sprawling and the young man wondered how the medicine man would decide which tree to pick. It was February and they all were bare and, to him, looked exactly the same, scattered aimlessly. A hawk was flying high overhead, making strange predatory sounds.

As they approached the orchard, William all of a sudden jumped straight up in the air and gave a bloodcurdling whoop that chilled the young man's spine. The medicine man then ran at a gallop right into the orchard and fell onto his face right in front of the tree that the young man knew gave the best fruit—the number one tree at the very center of the spiral.

He never figured out how the Navajo knew that was the best tree. There was no way he could have seen the pattern from ground level. But that tree became Henry Begay's tree and every year his clan would have the best apples in Shiprock.

"Want me to go tell those guys to stop all that shootin'?" the young man asked. There were still a lot of gunshots going off.

"No," Pa answered. "They're just young and stupid. Let 'em be." A gunshot sounded and he grunted and leaned forward in his rocking chair, his hand slowly falling to his lap. The pipe spilled, sending glowing embers over his pants

"Pa?" The young man got up from the porch steps and walked over to the slumped man. "You okay?" he asked and lifted the man's head. Then he saw the blood welling out of a small hole in Pa's chest and he pulled his father out of the chair and laid him gently on the porch. The old man was breathing heavily, gasping for breath. "Pa!" he yelled and cradled his head in his arms trying to do something—anything—to help him. The gunshots were moving farther away.

The young man was crying, frantic. His father coughed a few times and trembled in his son's arms. "Take it. . ." the old man gasped. "Take it to him. . ."

"What?" the young man cried through his tears. He had never known such sudden despair.

"You know. . ." his father whispered. "My life is over. . . Make it worthwhile. Take it to him." The words were but a rasp and almost silent.

"I'll get those guys, Pa. Don't die! I need you!" the young man choked.

"No." Only a whisper. "Take it to him."

For an hour the young man rocked on his knees, holding his limp and dead father in his arms, blood on the clothes of both of them, weeping at first uncontrollably and later silently.

Then he got up and walked inside the house and got a blanket. He placed his father's body on it. Later that night he carried the body out to the orchard. He was a big man and his father was small. He dug a grave near Henry's tree and buried the man who had raised and cared for him for twenty years. He used a rock for a gravestone and scratched a few words on it. He would do more later, but now he had a job to do.

It was almost dawn when he saddled up Hosteen and rode to the Foutz's trading post on the east side of Farmington, a couple of miles away. The Foutzes were awakening and he stopped outside the hogan where Billy Chee lived. Billy was the best leatherworker in Farmington. The young man woke him up and told him what he wanted and Billy said he'd have it ready the next morning. Billy sensed the desperation and intensity in the young man's eyes and knew that he would be paid for his work when it was picked up.

Then the young man rode back to his house and went to sleep. He slept all day and all night. Tomorrow he would fulfill his father's last request. Then he'd do something for himself.

~ ~ ~ ~

The young man awoke before dawn and packed provisions for his journey. He put the money that his father had stored in the house, about $80, in his pocket and saddled up Hosteen. He rode to the Foutz's trading post and Billy Chee had the saddlebags he wanted. He gave Billy $20 and placed the huge bags on Hosteen's rump. Billy knew Hosteen well and the bags fit perfectly.

Then he rode back to the house and stopped outside Pa's blacksmith's shop. He took the bags in and came out five minutes later with the bags filled. One was bulging and the other was about half filled. He placed them on Hosteen, who seemed to look proud to be carrying such a load. He fiddled a while with some other things he brought out from the shop and then rode back to the house. He left Hosteen at the front porch, where the horse shied away from the blood stain, and went inside. He came out with his father's Winchester rifle and a magazine and stood by Hosteen for a few minutes while he read. It was the June 1899 issue of *Scientific American,* the one they had last received. The rifle he placed in the holster on the right side of his saddle.

After a moment he put the magazine back in the house, locked up and led Hosteen to the back porch where he emptied the basket of apples for Henry Begay into the saddlebag that was half filled.

Then he and Hosteen headed north.

~ ~ ~ ~

The road from Farmington through Aztec, a little village on the Animas River, was practically empty and no one noticed the young man with the big horse and the almost comically bulging saddlebags. By afternoon he was headed north along the Animas up to Durango. He tried not to dwell on his father but on his quest.

He camped out right around the territory line about fifteen miles south of Durango. The land seemed to miraculously turn from the brown sage of New Mexico to the greenery of Colorado and he found a quiet spot by the Animas underneath a big bluff to the west.

The next morning early he was on his way and skirting Durango on the west when he heard a shout from his rear. He turned to see four men on horseback galloping towards him. He saw right away it was the Lords of Durango and his hand, perhaps not so instinctively, reached for his Winchester.

"Hands off that rifle, Farmington!" Jimerfield shouted and all four of the men drew their pistols and brandished them. "What are you doin' up here?" He had a big smile on his face, his two ferret teeth peeking out from his thin lips.

Tommy Beuten and Sid Leavell split apart from the others and approached him from the left. Jimerfield and Chuck—no one ever knew Chuck's last name—rode up to him on the right. The young man held his hands away from the rifle and stared with steely eyes at Jimerfield. "Let me go about my business," he said. He lowered his left hand behind him and there was a slight click that none of the gang heard.

Beuten said, "Them are some saddlebags you got there, Farmington. What's in 'em?" The young man remained silent.

Leavell moved his horse up to Hosteen and reached in the left saddlebag and brought out an apple. "Looky here!" he guffawed and took a bite. "Damn! That's pretty good." He said it with an unusual amount of sincerity that surprised his pals.

"Maybe we might have somethin' here," Chuck said, his long flowing yellow hair hanging down to his shoulders.

"Enjoy your apple and let me be," the young man said.

Jimerfield eyed him with interest and moved his horse closer to Hosteen on the right. "Well, Farmington, maybe we'll do that. But lemme see what you got in this one first." The black-shirted man reached down into the right saddlebag and immediately gave a howl that spooked all of the horses except Hosteen. He jerked his hand back and knocked his white hat off as all four of the men's horses whinnied in fear. Chuck fell off his horse and there was a sickening snap as his foot hit the ground. The three men stared at Jimerfield in horror. The gang leader's hair was standing straight out from his head like the thousand quills of a porcupine.

The young man snicked at Hosteen and they moved at a fast speed up the road north. Beuten and Leavell couldn't take their eyes off Jimerfield, whose gaped mouth seemed like it would never close. His eyes had rolled back up into his skull and his hair was slowly drifting down in its usual greasy state. Chuck was moaning on the ground.

~ ~ ~ ~

The young man stayed off the main road through Durango, instead taking the Florida road that branched around the mining town on the west. He camped that night in the high mountains north of Durango, about thirty miles south of the mining town of Silverton. He heard in the distance the narrow-gauge train that carried miners and ore between Durango on the south and Ouray on the north. The whistle and sound of the engine was calming to him, even though he knew nothing about mining, and cared less. He'd always wanted to ride the train with his Pa but the opportunity never arose. He'd heard that the scenery from the train was spectacular as it wound its way along the Animas.

It took him over a week to cross the Rocky Mountains and the Sangre de Christos and he'd never seen such sights. Occasionally he'd run across a small mining camp or a small ranch and a few of the people gave him some grub and let him rest for a spell. Everyone he met seemed curious about the huge saddlebags but were too polite to ask. In general, the pioneers of Colorado believed in minding their own business and letting you mind your own.

The last city before his goal was Cañon City and he decided to skip it. There was a territorial prison there and even the chance of seeing the huge gorge of the Arkansas River didn't tempt him. He'd read in *Harper's* that some crazy engineers had proposed building a span over the gorge, but no one really believed they would.

The young man and Hosteen continued on their quest.

~ ~ ~ ~

An hour before dawn, they crested the blue-traced ridge and he saw the most beautiful thing he'd ever seen, or imagined. Off to his left was a snow-capped peak that rose majestically up into the clouds, another just to the south of it. But catching his eyes and holding them was the valley floor below. It was a big valley, extending to the base of the peaks on the west and on into the horizon on the north and south. In the center of the valley was a grid of hundreds of blue dots, a shade of turquoise and cerulean he'd never seen before. In the crisp, cold and dry Colorado night the dots didn't twinkle like stars, they pulsated in a rigid north-south *straight* grid that was so unnatural in the Colorado wilderness that it made him gasp out loud.

The grid was almost a square, with about fifty dots across and fifty dots down, each uniformly spaced.

Hosteen drew back a step, instinctively. There was something utterly alien about the blue-dotted valley.

"We're almost there, Hosteen," the young man said and they slowly wended their way down the crest into the valley below.

An hour later the sun began to peek over the eastern horizon and the dots went out—all at once. The city of Colorado Springs had turned off its street lamps. Not the gas lamps used by all of the other cities of the civilized world—the electric lights supplied by the El Paso Power Company.

Four hours later the young man rode his horse to the east side of the city and began to approach the base of Pike's Peak that towered like a religious icon. He was almost there.

He met a few ranchers along the trip and one of them he asked directions. The rancher knew exactly what he was seeking and pointed the way. An hour later the young man followed a road that led to a huge metal fence and gate, behind which stood a tall, well-dressed man with a dark mustache and a smile on his face.

Nikola Tesla said, "I've been expecting you."

~ ~ ~ ~

After cleaning up in a nicely furnished house with amenities the young man had never heard of, he sat down with the great man he'd read of numerous times in *Scientific American.* Tesla had summoned an assistant who took care of Hosteen and unloaded the saddle bags carefully, taking them into a huge warehouse that stood beside the house.

"How can you have expected me?" the young man asked, in awe of the inventor.

"The mining towns of Colorado communicate a great deal," Tesla said, "and there was an amusing story about a gang of hooligans in Durango who were 'shocked' by a man from Farmington in the New

Mexico territory. The description of the way the man's hair stood up all around his head meant only one thing to me. You have one of my coils. Apparently a very efficient one, since it seems to be able to fit into a saddlebag."

The young man nodded his head, amazed at the deductive powers of the inventor. "Sherlock Holmes has nothing on you, Mr. Tesla."

"I very much want to see your coil. But one thing I cannot figure out is what you used for power. Surely to get such a reaction you must have had a huge power source?"

"I used leyden jars that my father made in his blacksmith shop. He's the one who made the coil, using some of the diagrams from *Scientific American."*

Tesla sat up straight and exclaimed, "But leyden jars cannot possibly supply such power."

"They are ordinary leyden jars—four of them in series. They're in the left saddlebag, under some apples. The coil is in the right saddle bag."

"I must see this coil. Right away." The inventor stood up and they walked quickly to the warehouse, which the young man saw was a huge laboratory of incredible machines. Some of the coils made him gasp at their size.

The young man pulled the coil out of the saddlebag, after disconnecting some wires that ran from the left bag to the right. It was a metal donut about 18 inches in diameter.

"A-a-a torus!" Tesla sputtered. "But I never designed any coils in the shape of a torus, and there were no diagrams of anything like *this* in the *Scientific American."*

"My pa was always experimenting around with the things he read. Always changing them and seeing what happens."

"I *must* meet your father— immediately!"

The young man looked towards the ground as he replied, "I'm sorry. He died. It was his last wish that I bring this to you. Ever since he read that you had moved to Colorado Springs he talked about us coming here to see you. But he was the blacksmith for Farmington and we never got the chance."

"A blacksmith." The mustached inventor's eyes misted and he said, "You must stay here with me, young man, and I will show you the wonders of technology. I may even show you how we will eventually communicate with Mars—and Jupiter."

The young man's mind reeled.

~ ~ ~ ~

For three days he stayed with Tesla and he saw sparks and lightning streaks of indescribable dimension. He saw machines that took his breath away, some of them literally as he felt the magnetic attraction of millions of volts. He had the grand tour of a lifetime guided by the greatest genius of the century.

But then he said he had to return to Farmington.

The inventor asked him to come with him to New York once his experiments with interplanetary communication in Colorado Springs were completed. But the young man declined. He must return to his home.

Tesla agreed, but insisted that he leave behind the three apples that were left. He thereafter told his friends in Paris and New York that the best apples he ever ate, even though they were beyond ripe, were from Farmington, in the new state of New Mexico.

~ ~ ~ ~

Ten days later Hosteen and the young man were moving leisurely down the Florida Road to the west of Durango when they heard gunfire. Carefully they moved into a copse of cottonwood trees and moved toward the shots. From behind the trees the young man looked out on a small glen where it looked as if an apple orchard had once stood. Someone had gone through a lot of trouble to uproot and destump the area and now there was a makeshift race track there. Cowboys were racing from right to left across the track and shooting their guns into the air at the end of each race.

He recognized the Lords of Durango. He watched for several races, noticing the girls that stood on the side of the track, cheering every winner, of which Jerry Jimerfield seemed to be the main one. Chuck, with his leg in a white cast, sat with the girls in a wooden chair. He shot his gun into the air at the end of every race too. There was a lot of hooting and hollering and all seemed to be having a grand time.

The young man placed a hand on his Winchester and thought how easy it would be to pick off one, or two, or maybe even all of the Lords of Durango by shooting them at the end of a race when the sounds of his rifle would be masked by the shooting of their guns. They probably wouldn't even notice anything was wrong until there were four bodies lying on the ground. And unless they saw his muzzle flash, they still wouldn't know where the shots came from.

But after watching a few more races he took his hand away from his rifle and pulled Hosteen away from the edge of the copse. He'd been away from Farmington long enough. The Taylors and the Nygrens probably had some horses to be shod, and there might still be some apples on some of the late-blooming trees. And Pa was a wise man. It wasn't what he wanted.

The young man rode on to Farmington.

There was a new century on the horizon and he hoped it would be less violent than the last.

THE MARTINGALE ARMS

A GAMBLING FABLE

THE FIVE POKER PLAYERS who had just finished their weekly Friday night session were sitting on the verandah looking out over the bay and drinking a final beer. The topic of conversation was gambling and the atmosphere was jovial. The host said, "Did I ever tell you guys about the Martingale brothers?"

A couple of the men shook their heads and the host continued, "It's the damnedest thing you ever heard. Fact, we wouldn't be sittin' here if it wasn't for those guys. Lemme tell you how it went."

THE MARTINGALE ARMS STORY

I guess it really started with old man Martingale. He made a small fortune in the publishing business and then up and died when his two sons, Abner and Zeke, were in their early 20s. About 15 years ago. Both of them were decent fellas, Abner more of a college guy and Zeke always trying to break into the business world without doing any real work himself. The old man, even though he had a bunch of money, never spoiled his kids. They had to work their own way and everybody seemed to respect the family for it.

Now this is just what I heard. I didn't come along till a bit later.

Anyway, at the reading of the will no one was very surprised when each of the boys was left half of the estate. The mother had died years back and there was only the two. Something like five million apiece.

Now this was right around the time when gambling was legalized in the state and a couple of small casinos opened up down by the beach. And it was also around the time when the city was worried about the homeless people who were showing up more and more around downtown.

Well, Abner knew right away what he wanted to do with his fortune. He wanted to help the homeless. So he approached Zeke and tried to get him to go in with him on some project that would give the homeless jobs and get them off the street. But Zeke wasn't having any of that. He also knew where he wanted his money to go—into one of them casinos. He wasn't a gambler, he just wanted to make a bunch of money by being a big casino mogul.

They argued a lot but it wasn't long before Zeke bought a big cut in one of the casinos, the Silver Dollar. Abner was disappointed, but Zeke told him that there was no way he was going to waste his money on homeless people. Not when there's plenty of money to be made on tourists and rich Hollywood people.

Abner just shook his head and said, "We'll see about that." That was when he got his big idea.

Now, you may remember that when gambling was legalized a lot of cities saw a gold mine in the casinos. They made so much money that the mayor and his crowd pushed through a bunch of tax levies on the casinos to pay for things the town needed. This wasn't unusual; most cities tax the hell out of the casinos and the casinos just shrug it off. They make so much money it's actually good publicity that they "support the community".

But Zeke didn't like the taxes at all. He didn't care about the city except as a place for his casino. But he wasn't about to buck the system and the Silver Dollar paid its taxes on time and in full.

So what did Abner do with his five mil? He ended up buying the old Strater Hotel, a few blocks away from the Silver Dollar. Big five-story apartment building with about 25 apartments. He got the building cheap, something like two million. It was empty and he put another million into fixing it up nice and about six months later he had an apartment house that anybody would want to live in—except maybe rich people who would want bigger rooms. The rooms were small but perfect for single people.

He called it the Martingale Arms. Then he started looking for people to move in. That was where the scheme started.

Abner put out the word that he wanted to rent to homeless people, but not just any homeless people. He screened every tenant.

Now I guess I ought to mention that one of the ways that the city spent the casino tax money was to subsidize housing and jobs for the homeless. If any company would give a job that paid at least $50 a day to a homeless person, the city would pay half of it. A few companies went for it but not many. Let's face it, not many of the homeless types were very skilled.

But Abner wanted only homeless people to live in his apartments and he'd offer the ones who applied—and there was a lot—a room and a $50-a-day job. A few of them, the ones who were good at it, worked around the building, cleaning it up, doing janitorial work, landscaping and stuff. They were glad to have the work and apparently they did a good job. It was a great place to live.

But the others got a different job offer: Here's what they had to do: gamble. In return for a room at the Martingale Arms he had them sign a contract that they would go to the Silver Dollar every day of the week and gamble. But they had to gamble *exactly* as he said. They would dress up nice—Abner provided each tenant with some decent clothes and laundry service until he could afford his own—and go to the casino and play roulette. Only roulette, which had no table limit and one green 0 spot. That was the Silver Dollar's big come-on, their no-limit roulette tables.

Here were Abner's instructions: you can bet on red or black, or odd or even, but *only* on red, black, odd or even. No numbers or any other options. You'll bet $50 on your first bet. As soon as you win once, you quit, collect your winnings—which was $50—and leave. If you lose, you double the bet to $100. If you lose again, you double the bet again. You keep doing this until you win, collect your $50 in winnings, and leave. If you lose sixteen times in a row, you leave the casino.

Abner explained to them that he had set up an account at the casino that each of his residents could tap into as needed if they went on a losing streak. Up to a million and a half, which is just about what they would be betting if they lost sixteen times in a row.

If anyone broke the rules, say by continuing to gamble after winning once, he'd fire them from the job and kick them out of the Martingale Arms. They were told this up front and in the ten years that the casino was in business only about a dozen people broke the rule. This went on until the Silver Dollar closed down about five years ago when a hurricane caused a bunch of damage.

Now the job only brought in $50 a day for the twenty tenants who gambled daily, and Abner charged them $10 a day rent, but that still left $280 a week profit for the residents, and that was good money for the typical homeless person, who didn't really have any other expenses. In fact, most of 'em ate at the casino and ate damn well. Fifteen years ago $280 a week was pretty good wages, especially for about fifteen minutes' work a day. Half of the twenty gamblers won on the first spin of the wheel and another half won on the next spin. Rarely did they have to go to the cage and get more money because they kept losing. They could walk over to the casino from the apartment house anytime they wanted, as long as they went once every 24 hours, and only once.

Abner even set up a group health insurance plan for every resident/worker and paid for it.

The Martingale Arms is still an apartment house now, but when the casino closed, Abner sold it to that Trump guy and moved to Florida. I hear he's helping out the homeless down there now. Zeke took his hurricane insurance money and his casino earnings and moved to the west coast somewhere.

And that's the story of the Martingale brothers.

One of the men on the verandah snorted, "Well, I'll be damned. How did that work? Nobody ever lost 16 times in a row?"

The host replied, "Figure it out yourself. The odds of losing sixteen 50-50 bets in a row is about 1 in 65,536, or maybe 60,000 because it's not quite a 50-50 bet. There's a green 0. Twenty guys going once a day would take about 3200 days to make that many bets, and that's about ten years. Abner was gambling that none of his 20 guys would go on a losing streak of sixteen in a row. And he lucked out and no one did.

"But even if one guy did, he could easily afford it. Look at what he was bringing in every year. The 25 tenants each paid him $70 a week rent and the city chipped in another $175. That's about a quarter million a year."

"But that would have meant he just broke even, if he had to cover for a guy who lost sixteen times in a row," another one of the men insisted. "Surely it cost him money to run the apartment house and pay taxes and stuff. And the health insurance for the tenants. . ."

"Oh it did," the host said, "Abner wasn't trying to make a lot of money. He just wanted the casino to pay the homeless people's salaries. When he sold the Martingale Arms for six million after 10 years he made all of his investment back, and more. But mainly he wanted his brother to support the hundreds of homeless people who came and went over the ten years the scheme was in operation. Zeke came out okay, but in reality *he* was the one who paid the salaries of the homeless people. Him and the taxpayers of the city."

One of the men said, "I never knew about this. Where the hell did you learn all this?"

The host smiled, "I was one of Abner's first tenants and I stayed for the whole ten years. How do you think I saved up enough for this place? I made $280 a week all that time and only spent it on food and books and, I have to admit, a few ladies. It was easy work and with compound interest I made out like a bandit. And I owe it all to Abner and Zeke. And the taxpayers, of course."

The five men each killed off their beers and went into the house, a six-room villa on the beach. Or as the host called it: "home".

AFTERWORD

In my previous book about Farmington New Mexico (THE TOTAH TRILOGY) I used the real names of the people I remembered from the 50s and 60s. The ones I didn't like didn't fare well in the stories. In THE NAKED TROCAR I used real people as my models but thinly disguised their names. I think I did this because many of the people in TROCAR are still alive and didn't fare well at all. In fact, they ended up as monsters.

Which is odd, because some of them were people I liked quite a bit back in the old days. Like Ben Eastburn (Barney Eastwick) and Larry Thrower (Lawrence T. Slinger). Larry was, and probably still is, such a strong, charismatic person that I don't worry about him being offended for being portrayed as a fat, murderous, necrophiliac sodomite. He's probably been called worse. Ben was a lawyer and a judge and is surely above being dragged down into a gripe about a book as inconsequential as this. He actually did represent me in a case very similar to the one in the story and we did triumph over a nefarious meter maid who was extremely pissed off about the decision.

Marty Jaynes is based on a real person and you could look up crimes of the 80s (or is it 70s) to find more particulars. I needed to use him in this story but I would prefer not to have anything to do with the real "Jaynes" if he's still alive. Nothing personal, but no thanks.

Anyone who's read Franklin W. Dixon should know who Detective Smuff is. It's the same guy the Hardy Boys used to bait and in my story he's used the same way.

The geography of my Farmington stories is as accurate as I can remember it; the history less so. There really is a Fat Man's Misery in Chokecherry Canyon and while it's not a dangerous as I make it out to be, if I were any heavier I wouldn't attempt it. I last climbed it in the late 90s. There was a mortuary in Shiprock—and maybe still is—but I have no idea where it was located.

I worked out most of the details of THE NAKED TROCAR while treadmilling at the hospital where I was treated for a heart attack back in May of 2007. I had a heart monitor during each session and it was amazing how well it worked. The cardiac tech monitoring me would invariably tell me to slow down because my heart rate was peaking *every* time I would mentally work something out with the plot. I guess the secret to keeping a low heart rate—at least for me—is to not be creative.

THE BEST REVENGE also owes a lot to my heart trouble. In April, while in California, I had a dream about a man from the "old west" meeting Nikola Tesla, a dream that was undoubtedly inspired by the 2006 Christopher Nolan film, THE PRESTIGE. I thought it might make a good story and had had a few ideas about how it would go when I had my heart attack. That night I was in ICU connected to all sorts of tubes and wires and there was no TV. I couldn't sleep because of the constant beeping of the monitors so I decided to think about the Tesla idea. During that long, long night I wrote practically every paragraph of the story in my mind. It only took about four hours to type it all in when I got out of the hospital. Can you tell?

The only real people in THE BEST REVENGE, besides Tesla, are the Lords of Durango and I'm pretty sure they won't mind being made into villains. Real musicians don't gripe about such things. They were my favorite band when I was getting started with my band in those days (1963 - 1967) and were called The Exotics. I used to go up to Durango every chance I would get to see them at the 3.2 beer joints up there and our band, The Torques, pretty much emulated them in every way. Played the same songs and picked the same licks.

In 1965 or 66 they went out to Hollywood to try to make it big and their agent changed their name to The Lords of London. They didn't get rich or famous but when they came back the stories they told about marijuana, LSD and sex probably changed more young lives in Durango and Farmington than did Johnson and Nixon combined.

Of course I know nothing about Farmington as it was at the start of the 20th century so all of that is simply made up. An article in the *Farmington Daily Times* mentioned that in those days the cowboys from Durango would come down and raise hell in Farmington from time to time, as I remember. That's it for my research.

THE MARTINGALE ARMS is a lagniappe—an old Louisiana tradition of giving a little something extra with every purchase—and was inspired by an article I read on the gambling strategy of "doubling down", also known as the Martingale Strategy. It seemed to me that under the right circumstances the strategy would work, and I proceed to lay out such a situation. Of course in real life it wouldn't work because a casino owner can kick you out of his joint for *any* reason. And he would if you tried something like this.

Thank you for reading this far. The ending of THE NAKED TROCAR seems to indicate that Knees Calhoon will not be returning to Farmington but don't you believe it. There are still a few skeletons in the San Juan County closet that merit the Calhoon treatment. Just let him replenish his stash and he'll make another visit—probably driving west at sundown.

RAMBLE HOUSE's

HARRY STEPHEN KEELER WEBWORK MYSTERIES

(RH) indicates the title is available ONLY in the RAMBLE HOUSE edition

The Ace of Spades Murder
The Affair of the Bottled Deuce (RH)
The Amazing Web
The Barking Clock
Behind That Mask
The Book with the Orange Leaves
The Bottle with the Green Wax Seal
The Box from Japan
The Case of the Canny Killer
The Case of the Crazy Corpse (RH)
The Case of the Flying Hands (RH)
The Case of the Ivory Arrow
The Case of the Jeweled Ragpicker
The Case of the Lavender Gripsack
The Case of the Mysterious Moll
The Case of the 16 Beans
The Case of the Transparent Nude (RH)
The Case of the Transposed Legs
The Case of the Two-Headed Idiot (RH)
The Case of the Two Strange Ladies
The Circus Stealers (RH)
Cleopatra's Tears
A Copy of Beowulf (RH)
The Crimson Cube (RH)
The Face of the Man From Saturn
Find the Clock
The Five Silver Buddhas
The 4th King
The Gallows Waits, My Lord! (RH)
The Green Jade Hand
Finger! Finger!
Hangman's Nights (RH)
I, Chameleon (RH)
I Killed Lincoln at 10:13! (RH)
The Iron Ring
The Man Who Changed His Skin (RH)
The Man with the Crimson Box
The Man with the Magic Eardrums
The Man with the Wooden Spectacles
The Marceau Case
The Matilda Hunter Murder
The Monocled Monster
The Murder of London Lew
The Murdered Mathematician
The Mysterious Card (RH)
The Mysterious Ivory Ball of Wong Shing Li (RH)
The Mystery of the Fiddling Cracksman
The Peacock Fan

The Photo of Lady X (RH)
The Portrait of Jirjohn Cobb
Report on Vanessa Hewstone (RH)
Riddle of the Travelling Skull
Riddle of the Wooden Parrakeet (RH)
The Scarlet Mummy (RH)
The Search for X-Y-Z
The Sharkskin Book
Sing Sing Nights
The Six From Nowhere (RH)
The Skull of the Waltzing Clown
The Spectacles of Mr. Cagliostro
Stand By—London Calling!
The Steeltown Strangler
The Stolen Gravestone (RH)
Strange Journey (RH)
The Strange Will
The Straw Hat Murders (RH)
The Street of 1000 Eyes (RH)
Thieves' Nights
Three Novellos (RH)
The Tiger Snake
The Trap (RH)
Vagabond Nights (Defrauded Yeggman)
Vagabond Nights 2 (10 Hours)
The Vanishing Gold Truck
The Voice of the Seven Sparrows
The Washington Square Enigma
When Thief Meets Thief
The White Circle (RH)
The Wonderful Scheme of Mr. Christopher Thorne
X. Jones—of Scotland Yard
Y. Cheung, Business Detective

Keeler Related Works

A To Izzard: A Harry Stephen Keeler Companion by Fender Tucker — Articles and stories about Harry, by Harry, and in his style. Included is a compleat Keeler bibliography.

Wild About Harry: Reviews of Keeler Novels — Edited by Richard Polt & Fender Tucker — 22 reviews of works by Harry Stephen Keeler from *Keeler News.* A perfect introduction to the author.

The Keeler Keyhole Collection: Annotated newsletter rants from Harry Stephen Keeler, edited by Francis M. Nevins

Fakealoo — Pastiches of the style of Harry Stephen Keeler by selected demented members of the HSK Society.

RAMBLE HOUSE's OTHER LOONS

The Julius Caesar Murder Case — A classic 1935 re-telling of the assassination by Wallace Irwin

The Contested Earth and Other SF Stories — A never-before published space opera and seven short stories by Jim Harmon.

Freaks and Fantasies — Eerie tales by Tod Robbins, collaborator of Tod Browning on the film FREAKS.

Vixen Scandal — Two sleaze masterpieces from the 60s by Jim Harmon: *Vixen Hollow* and *Celluloid Scandal.*

Maniac Siren — Two more sleaze marvels by Jim Harmon: *The Man Who Made Maniacs* and *Silent Siren*

West Texas War and Other Western Stories — by Gary Lovisi

Marblehead: A Novel of H.P. Lovecraft — A long-lost masterpiece from Richard A. Lupoff. Published for the first time!

The Secret Adventures of Sherlock Holmes — Three Sherlockian pastiches by the Brooklyn author/publisher, Gary Lovisi.

The Universal Holmes — Richard A. Lupoff's 2007 collection of five Holmesian pastiches and a recipe for giant rat stew.

Tales of the Macabre and Ordinary — Modern twisted horror by Chris Mikul, author of the *Bizarrism* series.

The Gold Star Line — Seaboard adventure from L.T. Reade and Robert Eustace.

The Werewolf vs the Vampire Woman — Hard to believe ultraviolence by either Arthur M. Scarm or Arthur M. Scram.

Black Hogan Strikes Again — Australia's Peter Renwick pens a tale of the outback.

Four Joel Townsley Rogers Novels — By the author of *The Red Right Hand: Once In a Red Moon, Lady With the Dice, The Stopped Clock, Never Leave My Bed*

Killing Time — New collection of short novels by Joel Townsley Rogers

Night of Horror — A short story collection of Joel Townsley Rogers

Twenty Norman Berrow Novels — *The Bishop's Sword, Ghost House, Don't Go Out After Dark, Claws of the Cougar, The Smokers of Hashish, The Secret Dancer, Don't Jump Mr. Boland!, The Footprints of Satan, Fingers for Ransom, The Three Tiers of Fantasy, The Spaniard's Thumb, The Eleventh Plague, Words Have Wings, One Thrilling Night, The Lady's in Danger, It Howls at Night, The Terror in the Fog, Oil Under the Window, Murder in the Melody, The Singing Room*

The N. R. De Mexico Novels — Robert Bragg presents *Marijuana Girl, Madman on a Drum, Private Chauffeur* in one volume.

Two Hake Talbot Novels — *Rim of the Pit, The Hangman's Handyman.* Classic locked room mysteries.

Two Alexander Laing Novels — *The Motives of Nicholas Holtz* and *Dr. Scarlett,* stories of medical mayhem and intrigue from the 30s.

Two Wade Wright Novels (and counting) — *Echo of Fear* and *Death At Nostalgia Street*, with more to come!

Three Rupert Penny Novels — *Policeman's Holiday, Policeman's Evidence* and *Sealed Room Murder,* classic impossible mysteries.

Five Jack Mann Novels — Strange murder in the English countryside. *Gees' First Case, Nightmare Farm, Grey Shapes, The Ninth Life, The Glass Too Many.*

Four Max Afford Novels — *Owl of Darkness, Death's Mannikins, Blood on His Hands* and *The Dead Are Blind* by One of Australia's finest novelists.

Five Joseph Shallit Novels — *The Case of the Billion Dollar Body, Lady Don't Die on My Doorstep, Kiss the Killer, Yell Bloody Murder, Take Your Last Look.* One of America's best 50's authors.

The Best of 10-Story Book — edited by Chris Mikul, over 35 stories from the literary magazine Harry Stephen Keeler edited.

The Anthony Boucher Chronicles — edited by Francis M. Nevins Book reviews by Anthony Boucher written for the *San Francisco Chronicle,* 1942 – 1947. Essential and fascinating reading.

A Young Man's Heart — A forgotten early classic by Cornell Woolrich

Muddled Mind: Complete Works of Ed Wood, Jr. — David Hayes and Hayden Davis deconstruct the life and works of a mad genius.

My First Time: The One Experience You Never Forget — Michael Birchwood — 64 true first-person narratives of how they lost it.

The Incredible Adventures of Rowland Hern — Rousing 1928 impossible crimes by Nicholas Olde.

Don Diablo: Book of a Lost Film — Two-volume treatment of a western by Paul Landres, with diagrams. Intro by Francis M. Nevins.

The Charlie Chaplin Murder Mystery — Movie hijinks by Wes D. Gehring

The Koky Comics — A collection of all of the 1978-1981 Sunday and daily comic strips by Richard O'Brien and Mort Gerberg, in two volumes.

Gamefinger — Incredible 1966 sado-sleaze from Clyde Allison (William Knoles).

Dime Novels: Ramble House's 10-Cent Books — *Knife in the Dark* by Robert Leslie Bellem, *Hot Lead* and *Song of Death* by Ed Earl Repp, *A Hashish House in New York* by H.H. Kane, and five more.

Stakeout on Millennium Drive — Indianapolis Noir — Ian Woollen.

Dope Tales #1 — Two dope-riddled classics; *Dope Runners* by Gerald Grantham and *Death Takes the Joystick* by Phillip Condé.

Dope Tales #2 — Two more narco-classics; *The Invisible Hand* by Rex Dark and *The Smokers of Hashish* by Norman Berrow.

Dope Tales #3 — Two enchanting novels of opium by the master, Sax Rohmer. *Dope* and *The Yellow Claw.*

Tenebrae — Ernest G. Henham's 1898 horror tale brought back.

The Singular Problem of the Stygian House-Boat — Two classic tales by John Kendrick Bangs about the denizens of Hades.

The One After Snelling — Kickass modern noir from Richard O'Brien.

The Sign of the Scorpion — 1935 Edmund Snell tale of oriental evil.

The House of the Vampire — 1907 thriller by George S. Viereck.

An Angel in the Street — Modern hardboiled noir by Peter Genovese.

The Devil's Mistress — Scottish gothic tale by J. W. Brodie-Innes.

The Lord of Terror — 1925 mystery with master-criminal, Fantômas.

The Lady of the Terraces — 1925 adventure by E. Charles Vivian.

My Deadly Angel — 1955 Cold War drama by John Chelton

Prose Bowl — Futuristic satire — Bill Pronzini & Barry N. Malzberg .

Satan's Den Exposed — True crime in TorC New Mexico — Award-winning journalism by the Desert Journal.

The Amorous Intrigues & Adventures of Aaron Burr — by Anonymous — Hot historical action.

I Stole $16,000,000 — True story by cracksman Herbert E. Wilson.

The Black Dark Murders — Vintage 50s college murder yarn by Milt Ozaki, writing as Robert O. Saber.

Sex Slave — Potboiler of lust in the days of Cleopatra — Dion Leclerq.

You'll Die Laughing — Bruce Elliott's 1945 novel of murder at a practical joker's English countryside manor.

The Private Journal & Diary of John H. Surratt — The memoirs of the man who conspired to assassinate President Lincoln.

Dead Man Talks Too Much — Hollywood boozer by Weed Dickenson

Red Light — History of legal prostitution in Shreveport Louisiana by Eric Brock. Includes wonderful photos of the houses and the ladies.

Gadsby — A lipogram (a novel without the letter E). Ernest Vincent Wright's last work, published in 1939 right before his death.

A Snark Selection — Lewis Carroll's *The Hunting of the Snark* with two Snarkian chapters by Harry Stephen Keeler — Illustrated by Gavin L. O'Keefe.

Ripped from the Headlines! — The Jack the Ripper story as told in the newspaper articles in the *New York* and *London Times.*

Geronimo — S. M. Barrett's 1905 autobiography of a noble American.

The Compleat Calhoon — All of Fender Tucker's works: Includes *The Totah Trilogy, Weed, Women and Song* and *Tales from the Tower,* plus a CD of all of his songs.

www.ingramcontent.com/pod-product-compliance
Lightning Source LLC
LaVergne TN
LVHW050937080826
845145LV00004B/1304

9781605430164